THE STRAY

Betsy James Wyeth

THE
STRAY

—— WITH DRAWINGS BY ——

Jamie Wyeth

FARRAR · STRAUS · GIROUX *New York*

Text copyright © 1979 by Betsy James Wyeth
Illustrations copyright © 1979 by Jamie Wyeth
Published simultaneously in Canada
by McGraw-Hill Ryerson Ltd., Toronto
Printed in the United States of America by A. Hoen
Bound by A. Horowitz and Sons
Designed by Harriett Barton
First edition, 1979

Library of Congress Cataloging in Publication Data
Wyeth, Betsy James. The stray.
[1. Animals—Fiction] I. Wyeth, James. II. Title.
PZ7.W9737St [Fic] 79-19344 ISBN 0-374-37280-2

FOR JAMIE

Contents

THE STRAY

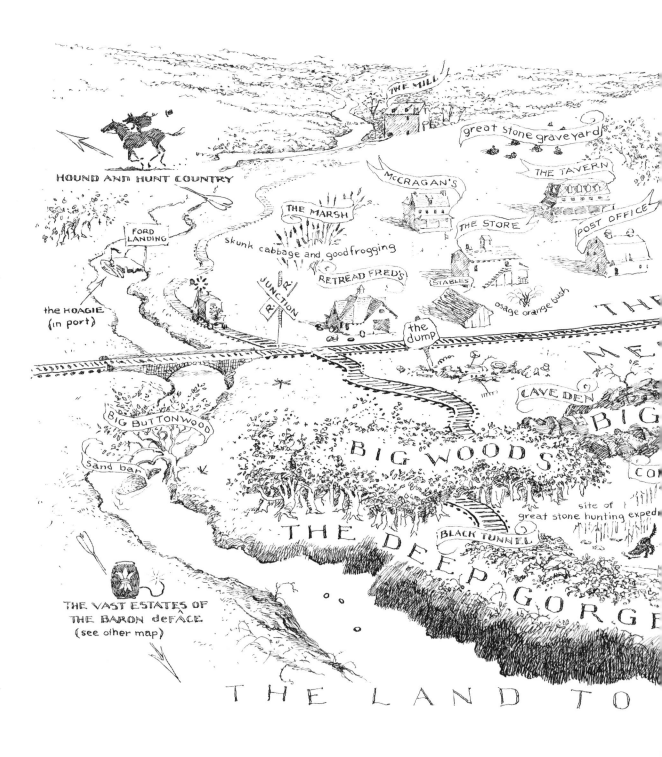

THE MILL

great stone graveyard

HOUND AND HUNT COUNTRY

McCRAGAN'S

THE TAVERN

THE MARSH

THE STORE

POST OFFICE

FORD LANDING

skunk cabbage and good frogging

RETREAD FRED'S

STABLES

the HOAGIE (in port)

JUNCTION

the dump

osage orange bush

THE

ME

CAVE DEN

BIG

BIG BUTTONWOOD

Sand bar

BIG WOODS

CO

site of
great stone hunting exped

THE DEEP

BLACK TUNNEL

THE VAST ESTATES OF
THE BARON deFACE
(see other map)

GORGE

THE NORTH

ROUNDELAY

DENTON'S HOLLOW

THE LAND BY THE SEA
WHERE BOOM·BOOM WAS BORN

BIG KARL'S

THE HILL

OW

THE GRANGE

OCKS

THE ROYAL PALACE
AFTER THE CROWNING·BLOW AFFAIR

ELD

THE FRD

THE PINES

BOOM TOWN

COMPILED BY
WIDDOES

CHARTED BY
ADMIRAL DEL

town line fence

THE SOUTH

DRAWN BY
ME

Lynch

It was raining the day Lynch arrived at the Ford. No one was around. He told me later that he thought it was a ghost town, and I can understand why. All of us were over at the Graveyard, near the Grange. Something terrible had happened and everyone who lived at the Ford had been shocked into the realization that the peace and quiet of our Village was threatened. For some time we had been aware of new sounds echoing across the hills, but they seemed so distant we hadn't given them much thought. Then one day Fox Glove's husband failed to return home to Denton's Hollow. We searched everywhere for him—along the River banks, up in the Big Rocks, down in the Marsh—and gave up only after we had covered every inch of the Big Woods without finding a trace.

He got back to the store and there was Lynch in a rocking chair on the front porch, acting like he owned the place. Kind Tink could see this stray was pretty thin and scraggy—he looked as though he'd been walking the tracks for a long time. Without any questions, Kind Tink invited him in for a bite to eat. Kind Tink was always throwing away store bills and taking in strays. It was through his warmheartedness that many strays found homes at the Ford. He let them live in the shacks and houses he owned and never charged a nickel for rent.

After a few days, when it began to look like Lynch wasn't in any hurry to move on down the tracks, Kind Tink thought things over and decided to ask Toots if she would look after him. Toots was another one of Kind Tink's strays. She lived in one of his houses up in the Big Rocks that run along the Valley ridge. He knew Toots was pretty lonely up there waiting for her sweetheart, Engineer Flaherty, to return. He had dropped her off at the Junction, saying he'd be back someday to pick her up. So, while she was waiting, arrangements were made for Lynch to live with her.

We never asked Lynch where he came from and he never talked about his past. He just came into our lives like cloud shadows passing over the Hill—illusive, fleeting, not easy to catch or pin down. I don't mean Lynch was wishy-washy. Anything but. He was tough, independent, clever, full of the daredevil, and not held down by anything. He didn't exactly set out to break the rules of the Ford, he just never seemed to notice them.

At first, Lynch didn't hang around the Village, so it was a while before we met. When I finally saw him, he was on wheels. Lynch had a passion for anything that would move. He had a knack for rigging up crazy contraptions that somehow always worked. That particular day, I was over picking strawberries on the Hill. Intent on picking, I glanced up and saw something flying down the Hill out of control and heading straight for me. I jumped up. Strawberries flew in six directions as the object on wheels went careening toward a pile of rocks. There was a terrible crash. Amid a tangle of spinning wheels and splintered

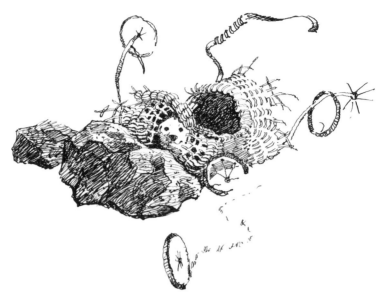

wicker was Lynch, grinning sheepishly. He said that, poking around the Dump, he'd found a broken-down baby carriage, oiled up the wheels, pushed it through the fields, climbed in, and given it a test run down the Hill.

The better I got to know him, the more I envied his carefreeness, which even included his clothes. He never had a nickel to his name, so had learned to make do without. He wasn't too proud to wear every assortment of cast-off jackets, hats, and shoes. You never knew what odd, mismatched outfit he'd come up with. It might be an army jacket over a pair of sailor's pants. The next time, he would have on a frontiersman's shirt and be wearing a broad-brimmed hat. His pride and joy was his black leather Road Knight's outfit, complete with dark glasses. It was the only clothing we ever saw Lynch buy. He earned the money by selling honey.

Using his ingenuity, he figured out a way to find a honey tree.

First he lured a bee into a matchbox full of moistened sugar. He let the bee lap up its fill; then, watching which direction it flew in, he ran hell-bent after it until the bee disappeared from sight.

Sliding open the matchbox again, he lured another bee, and ran after it. Six bees later, Lynch found a great hollow tulip poplar tree standing smack in the middle of the Big Woods. Lynch was sure it was full of honey, and he was right. He sold paper cup after paper cup full of that honey, until he had enough money to send away for the black leather Road Knight's outfit.

Lynch and I hit it off right away, but he took a dim view of my friend McCragan and all his polite Village ways. McCragan's mother was a dressmaker, and evidently a good one. Word had spread beyond the Ford that she could make any sort of outfit for any sort of occasion, and to top it off, she was cheap. That's when strangers other than strays began sneaking into the Ford. She had more business than she could handle, so McCragan was his mother's helper when he wasn't working at the Store. He was born with manners. He was just the opposite of a type like Lynch, who would never be pinned down to a routine. McCragan actually enjoyed meeting these customers from far away when they came to have a dress or a jacket made. It gave him a chance to show off his charm. He would hold the pins while his mother shortened or lengthened a skirt or sleeve. He'd bring them cups of tea if a fitting took too long and they grew faint. And he listened to their gossip about the Land to the North, where someone lived who kept stables full of Hunters and kennels overflowing with baying hounds.

None of us realized how important this information would be one day. For the time being, I just was disappointed that my two friends didn't seem to like each other. The Grange meeting changed all that.

Not long after Toots moved to the Ford, she started attending meetings at the Grange, and finally went through initiation to become a real member. She wanted the same for Lynch, for, after all, both of them were strays, and there had never been much time for joining clubs or becoming a member of a grange. Lynch flatly refused and said that gatherings gave him the creeps. He loved to interrupt meetings by stealing up close to the Grange and moaning like a ghost outside.

Nobody paid any attention to him, but then he went a step too far. Toots had been asked to recite her poem about the Dove of Peace. She had talked Lynch into releasing a white pigeon through the small trapdoor in the ceiling of the Grange—it was supposed to flutter around the room. Her signal to Lynch would be the words "And the Dove of Peace flew round about." The moment arrived. Toots's voice rang out, but nothing happened. Once more she said, "And the Dove of Peace flew round about." Still, nothing happened.

Finally, on the third try, the trapdoor opened, but instead of the white pigeon, Lynch's head appeared, covered with soot and cobwebs. "Toots, I guess the cat caught the Dove of Peace. Should I throw down the cat instead?"

The meeting broke up with roars of laughter and poor Toots never finished reciting her poem. When she got back to the Big Rocks she gave Lynch the tanning of his life and made him promise he would become a member of the Grange. Of course he skipped out on most of the preliminary meetings, and I never dreamed he'd turn up on the big day. I sneaked into the Grange and took my place in the back row. There, sitting up in the

front row alongside Toots, was Lynch, all wrapped up in a
white sheet. We sang a few songs and then it was time for Lynch
to walk up onto the stage to go through the initiation ceremony.
He stood there self-conscious in his white sheet, when suddenly
the stage curtains parted and a head peered through way up high.
It was a monster, complete with fangs that dripped blood, with
crossed eyes, and pointed ears and head. In half a minute the

Grange was cleared, everyone running in six directions, with Lynch in the lead—sheet flapping as he ran. He disappeared up over the Hill. A posse was organized, but they never found a trace of the monster. I had a pretty good idea who it was, but Lynch didn't find out who had saved him from the dreaded initiation until one rainy day when we all went over to the Grange, where a chest full of costumes for plays was kept. Mc-Cragan opened a box of dried-up theatrical makeup. He softened the nose putty, deftly applied the makeup, threw a black cape over his shoulders, and there before our eyes was the monster. From that day forward, Lynch and McCragan were fast friends. He never appeared at a Grange meeting again, for Toots saw it was more trouble than she could handle.

Den Den

One day Lynch and I were out hacking around waiting until McCragan finished his work at the Store. McCragan had to help support his mother, so on Saturdays he bagged groceries and did odd jobs for Kind Tink.

We decided to kill time until he was through by walking the tracks. Lynch kept talking about his plans for completing a contraption that could run on the tracks, and I wasn't thinking about anything much at all. Without realizing it, we had walked across the Town Line and were on the other side, where the tracks ran smack through a farm located at the bottom of the Hill, which was the eastern boundary of the Ford. Everyone said it was owned by an unfriendly farmer who came from a foreign land. We were just about to start back when Lynch spotted something. The next thing I knew, he was racing across the fields toward the farm's big garden. Panic-stricken, I yelled to warn him that someone was coming around the end of the barn with a shotgun, but it was too late. I heard the shotgun blast as I turned, and ran pell-mell back down the tracks toward the Ford.

This was the first time since before the funeral I had crossed over the Town Line, and I remembered with panic what had happened to Fox Glove's husband, but when I reached the Big Rocks and caught my breath I began to feel sort of guilty for running back home and leaving Lynch. In times of panic or distress, Lynch, McCragan, and I had a secret signal—three crow caws. I cawed three times and listened, but no crow caws came back from Lynch. Over and over again I cawed, until I reached the top of the Hill, where I could look down to see if Lynch was anywhere in sight. What I saw ended all hope for Lynch: the enclosed barnyard was full of wagons, which had been hidden from view when we were on the tracks. I turned back to spread the alarm and then I heard something—three crow caws coming up from the farm below. Overjoyed, I cawed back, threw all caution to the wind, ran down the Hill, crossed over the Town Line and into the farmyard.

Lynch met me at the farmhouse door and said, "Come on in and meet Big Karl."

When I stepped inside, the farmhouse turned out to be a giant smokehouse with thick, whitewashed stone walls. Kegs of cider and beer sat on the cool entryway floor, and I could hear the sound of hearty laughter coming from somewhere. Without a word, Lynch opened a door to the kitchen, where smoked hams and links of sausage hung from ceiling hooks, while whole cabbages bubbled in big pots on the stove. I was introduced to Big Karl and his guests. They were seated around tables, roaring with laughter, drinking mugs of beer

and cider, and talking. We listened while they told stories about a brutal raider from the Old Country nicknamed Sour Kraut who ravaged the countryside until in the end Big Karl and his friends were forced to flee across the Sea to start life anew in our Valley.

I often wonder how different things would have been if we hadn't crossed over the Town Line and met Big Karl. On that first visit, however, all I could think about was getting back to the Ford and finding out if anyone had heard the shotgun blast. But Lynch wouldn't budge. He knew I was worried, but he just grinned and kept asking more questions about Sour Kraut. Big Karl told us his nickname came from his passion for hot dogs with sauerkraut. He had been born in a thatched sty with an earthen floor on some Duke's country estate located in the Old Country. From the beginning, Sour Kraut's ideas of climbing up the social ladder were hindered by his humble, earthen-floor background. He never attended the local schools but spent all his time boar hunting instead and became such a ruthless boar killer that the Duke sent for him. In no time at all, the walls of the Duke's hunting lodge were lined with boars' heads. When the Boar War broke out, the Duke chose Sour Kraut to head his army, and that's when Big Karl and his friends fled across the Sea to start anew.

Victory after victory enriched the Duke's treasure box (which was strapped in gold), until one day Sour Kraut vanished over the border, taking the Duke's treasure box with him. No one knew if he was hiding in the mountains or had crossed the Sea and was living in our land. Just to be on the safe side, Big Karl kept a shotgun for protection, which explained why he fired a warning shot when he spotted Lynch running across his fields.

Finally Lynch stood up to leave, and said, "Is she still asleep?"

Big Karl walked over to a box in the corner, reached in, lifted out a bundle, and handed it to Lynch. I looked inside the bundle and saw a piglet fast asleep. She had pink ears and a crooked snout that leaned way over to the left.

The piglet was what Lynch had spotted in Big Karl's garden and dashed across his fields to save. He told me he knew she was a stray because of the way she was nibbling on a big head of cabbage. No one must see her, as we didn't want to explain where we got her. We decided there was only one place to hide her and that was in our Cave Den we had up in the Big Rocks. We fixed her up with a bed of straw and blocked the Cave Den entrance with a low board. I was sure she would start whimpering when we left her alone for the first time, but I was wrong. We listened and in a few minutes we could hear her contented snores coming from inside.

McCragan was a little miffed because he'd missed all the excitement, but when we took him up to the Cave Den to see the piglet, he melted and gave her a name, Den Den. It was fairly easy to keep Den Den a secret while she was small, but soon she began to grow and grow. We had trouble keeping her confined. One night I was awakened by three crow caws coming from the tree outside my window. It was Lynch. Den Den had knocked down the board in front of the Cave Den entrance and was gone. We spent a sleepless night searching for her.

In the morning, McCragan looked out of his window and almost fainted when he saw Den Den sitting in the rocker on the Store porch. He held his breath as he spotted Kind Tink coming down the lane to open up the Store. Kind Tink walked up the stairs, opened the door, and Den Den followed him inside. All that McCragan could think of was those shelves of food, those bins full of vegetables, and those cakes and cookies. Den Den had developed an enormous appetite and he knew she'd never seen so much food. He expected the worst, but breathed a sigh of relief when back out the door came Den Den, loaded down with bags of groceries. Kind Tink thought he'd found a new stray. It was as simple as that. McCragan sauntered over in his most casual way and inquired where this new stray would be setting up housekeeping. Kind Tink looked worried and said he'd run out of houses. Did McCragan have a spare room in his house?

"No, but don't give her another thought. I'll find a place for her up in the Big Rocks."

By the end of summer, Den Den was enormous. She was so bored that all she did was eat and eat and eat. Nothing fit her, and she couldn't run around the Ford without some sort of clothes. Then there was the matter of her bad temper. We humored her as best we could by tickling her right foreleg. You could work her out of the meanest temper tantrum by tickling under that foreleg while she rolled on the ground, dissolved in grunting laughter, but it was only a temporary solution to the problem of keeping her busy. We ended up by appointing her Stationmaster of the Ford. McCragan found an old station-master's hat, pinned a badge above the visor, and hung a whistle around her neck. Den Den kept all our switches clear. But very few trains stopped at the Ford, which meant she had a lot of spare time on her hands to poke her crooked snout into this and that.

A new Den Den problem concerned the customers that came to McCragan's house for fittings. Den Den looked these strangers over and took an instant dislike to them. She kept calling them stuck-up. Perhaps she was jealous of their fancy clothes and social airs, or maybe their very long, very straight noses bothered her —anyway, whenever one came to McCragan's house for a fitting, Den Den would press her crooked snout right up against the window and peer in to watch, never taking her eyes off the stranger. Sometimes she would even mutter threats under her breath, which, needless to say, made those customers extremely nervous. They warned McCragan's mother that if that creature with the crooked snout and stationmaster's hat kept up this peering business they would never come back. We tried to reason with Den Den, but there was absolutely no way to talk her out of her dislikes. The situation was becoming serious. When customers from the Land to the North came into the Ford, they turned right around and headed back without stopping if Den Den was anywhere in sight.

New Job

Lynch came to the rescue. He'd been gone for two or three whole days and we were beginning to think he had moved on down the tracks, when he showed up with a strange tale about the Land to the South. It seems that for a long time Lynch had been curious about the other side of the River. Without saying anything to anyone, he crossed the River on the railway trestle in the dead of the night and started walking south along the River banks on the forbidden side. Sure enough, before long he ran smack into a fence. He lit a match. Nailed to the fence was a sign that said: KEEP OFF, signed *Baron deFâce*. Undaunted, Lynch wiggled through an opening in the fence. On and on he walked through the dark woods that came down to the River banks. At the first sight of dawn he made out what looked like a great height of land ahead. The daredevil in Lynch came out. He left the River and worked his way up the side of a Deep Gorge. When he reached the top, he walked to the edge of the forest and saw on a distant hill a huge castle with banners flying from a turret in the morning breeze. We didn't believe his story. Lynch said, "Want to bet?"

McCragan was smart and backed off, but I said, "I'll bet you a quarter you can't prove it."

Lynch grinned from ear to ear and took out of his pocket an ad some River rat had given him. It read:

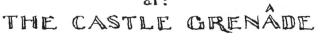

WANTED
a stationmaster
for ^A
BARON de FACE'S
PRIVATE RAILWAY

direct all inquiries
to:
the estate manager
at:
THE CASTLE GRENÂDE ^A

There it was in plain black and white, the Castle Grenâde. Lynch was strutting around like a proud peacock while we pretended we really *had* believed him from the start. Unfortunately,

Den Den was close by. She overheard Lynch's description of the Castle and demanded we read her the ad. We never should have, because, from that moment on, all we heard night and day was "castle—castle—castle." We tried to reason with her that to take a stationmaster's job in such a faraway, unknown land not only meant she would have to leave the Ford, but it was dangerous. We reminded her about those mysterious explosions, which didn't seem to faze her one bit. So we decided the only thing to do, since she couldn't write, was to send in an application, assuring ourselves she would never qualify, but at least maybe we would have some peace.

A week later the Estate Manager turned up at the Ford Landing. Den Den was so overawed at the sight of his elegant uniform and pistol in a holster that she just stood speechless and batted her long blond eyelashes in a coy way. To our amazement, the Estate Manager winked back, so Lynch went into action to show the Estate Manager her other side. He stepped behind a big Osage orange bush that grew by the Store and began saying over and over, "Den Den has a crooked snout. Den Den has a crooked snout." Then he ran to beat the wind for cover in a shed close by. Den Den exploded and bellowed out her instant rage. She began pawing the ground to set her mark, muttering between snorts, "A-one and a-two and a-three and a-four. On your mark, get set—GO!"

This was the sign for her most violent attacks. The Estate

Manager, McCragan, and I ran for shelter as she charged that Osage orange bush, ripping it up, roots and all; wheeling around, she charged again. When the dust settled, the Estate Manager hired Den Den on the spot. Lynch had misjudged. It was love at first sight.

Before she left, we gave her a big going-away party at the Tavern. Everyone was invited. Instead of sending out invitations, for fear someone might be overlooked, we lettered three big posters: one for the Post Office, one for the Store, and the third for the Tavern. They said:

ALL FOR ONE——ONE FOR ALL

COME TO A GOODBYE PARTY

FOR DEN DEN

AT THE TAVERN

SIX-THIRTY

NEXT SATURDAY NIGHT

FLOOD OR FULL MOON

McCragan was in charge of the decorations, while Lynch and I took up a collection for the extras. The Tavern Keeper gave us a special price on the food. McCragan's mother made Den Den a flowered muumuu, but had to hide it after the final fitting, because Den Den kept teasing to wear the only dress she had ever owned. The rooms at the Tavern looked beautiful. McCragan had hung Japanese lanterns and put candles on the tables, with big bouquets of field flowers and dishes of acorns. The centerpiece on the main table was a huge cabbage.

The guests began arriving at a quarter after six. Miss Den Den was standing in the hall, receiving. I couldn't believe my eyes. McCragan's mother had taken her in hand and given Den Den what looked to be a permanent. There she was, all dressed up in

her flowered muumuu, a corsage of carrots, radishes, turnips, and parsley pinned to one shoulder, and her head covered with curls. She had mascara on her long, bleached eyelashes, and a sunflower tucked behind her ear. She even had attempted lipstick. It started out just fine, then disappeared at a strange angle up her crooked snout.

Things were rather stiff at first but loosened up after the cider began to flow. The crowded Tavern rooms hummed and buzzed and eventually roared. Stepping outside for some fresh air, I made a wish on the first evening star that Den Den would like her new job. The band arrived just before dinner was served. In came platters of turnips, carrots, cabbages, wild rice that grew in the Marsh, peas, and the treat of treats, lemon-meringue pies.

After dinner the old Tavern rocked with the stomping of many feet and roaring laughter, and in the middle of it all, Den Den was dancing the Highland fling!

The next time I saw her, the crowd had made a large circle around two dancing, bobbing figures, while everyone stomped to keep time. In the center of the large circle was Den Den, doing the polka with Big Karl! That's when I realized she had on a wig; it had slipped forward and dangled over one ear.

When we talked the party over the next day, Lynch told us how he had gone out to the back shed to refill a pitcher of cider and found him peeking longingly through a window at the festivities going on inside. On the back-shed floor sat basket after basket full of cabbages, with a note that said, "Good luck, Den Den, from your friend Big Karl." He had heard about the party, but since his farm was outside the Town Line, he didn't feel included in the invitation. Lynch realized how thoughtless we had been, so he brought Big Karl in.

The Sunday train pulled into the Ford a little after noon. Den Den stood at the side of the tracks, still wearing her flowered muumuu and a trace of lipstick. The mascara had washed away from so much laughing and so many goodbye tears, and the blond wig was lost, trampled underfoot the night before. Far down the Valley, the train's whistle echoed, announcing her coming departure. We loaded Den Den on board, along with all those baskets of cabbages. When she waved from the back of the caboose, everyone began to cry. Just before the train disappeared around the bend, Den Den reached down in her satchel, took out her old stationmaster's hat, and put it on her head. A salute to her past with us at the Ford and to her future in the Land to the South.

Every now and then, Lynch would bring us bits of news from that mysterious Estate of the Baron deFâce. Den Den was a huge success. Den Den had fallen in love and married the Estate Manager. We sent her a message of congratulations, but of course never heard a word in reply.

Boom Boom

Shortly after Den Den left, the whole Valley became terrorized by the appearance of a large creature first seen swimming in the River. It became known as the Black Monster. Two villagers were in their boat, fishing, when the Black Monster appeared from nowhere, swimming alongside. It put a great hairy, black paw on the gunwale and capsized the boat. Terrified villagers swam frantically for shore. Next it was seen up in the Cornfield digging

crater-like holes. Holes large enough to bury a body in. In the meadow were mysterious piles of stones put there as if to mark graves. It was no longer safe to camp along the River banks. In the dead of night, the Black Monster might stick its head through the tent flaps. Tent after tent was abandoned as the frightened

occupants fled for safety in the night. When they returned in the morning, their tents were gone. Some said the Black Monster frothed at the mouth. Others swore it had bared its teeth. All agreed on one thing—it had a voice like a booming cannon.

Before we knew it, fall had slipped away and the drifting snows of winter had arrived. The worst blizzard of the winter was raging. The north wind had been blowing snow down on us since early morning. After supper, I pulled my chair up close to the fireplace and thought how snug everything was, glad to be inside while the howling wind sounded like freight trains passing in the night. I thought I heard a knock at the door but knew no one would be out in this storm. It must be a loose shutter bracket. Then another knock.

When I opened the door, something that looked like a snow-bank was standing there. Then a tongue came out. Eyes blinked. It was Lynch! There was an emergency. Fox Glove was missing. Fox Glove, who still lived up in Denton's Hollow, had two young ones to rear all by herself after her husband was killed. It would be insane to go out searching for her in this blizzard, and I had a hard time convincing Lynch not to go back to the Big Rocks that night. Several times I wakened to see him pacing the floor or putting another log on the fire. He didn't sleep a wink. It was a long night.

At dawn we looked out on our world transformed into white. Lynch and I were off on the search, not even stopping to eat breakfast. Only the tops of a few dry corn shucks rattled in the wind when we crossed the Cornfield, calling, calling, calling. There was no reply, nor could we find any tracks in the snow. We were nearing the Town Line fence, which was the southern boundary of the Ford, when who should come tripping lightly across the top of the deep snow but Fox Glove!

She told us that the morning before, when it first began to snow, she had started out to catch a mess of field mice for her young ones. That was one of the best times to go mousing. She had been right. The mousing was good, but before she knew it, there was the Town Line. Not being able to resist, she reached under the Town Line fence for one last fat mouse she spotted on the other side. She caught the mouse, but in turning back, she got her long tail tangled up in the fence. Try as hard as she could to free her tail, matters only got worse. She began to panic. Her mouse bag fell on the snow—freed mice scampered back to their burrows.

The snow got deeper and deeper and Fox Glove was numb with cold. She was afraid of falling into the final sleep of deep cold, and kept her spirits up by singing, until she was just a snowy lump with a frail song coming from within. At first she thought she was dreaming when, through the raging blizzard, she heard a booming cannon. Then two huge black paws dug down to reach her under the snow. Towering over her was the Black Monster! He licked her face with a long red tongue, then curled up beside her. Warmth slowly came back into her frozen limbs. All through that long night, the creature stayed by Fox Glove.

In the morning, the Black Monster dug down furiously in the deep snow, tearing and biting and yanking until he pulled up the Town Line fence, post and all, and freed Fox Glove's tail.

We walked her safely back, got a bite of breakfast, and started out once more in the direction of the Town Line. Sure enough, there was the Town Line fence in a shambles, with a big hunk of Fox Glove's fur caught in the barbed wire. Giant paw prints led into the unknown lands. We took a chance and followed their trail. That led us to the Pines. Sitting all alone on the edge of the Pines, looking like a huge hairy boulder, was the Black Monster. I hesitated, but not Lynch. Smart Lynch whistled and called out, "Hey, Black Monster!" No answer. "Hey, Monster." The boulder never moved. "Hey, Friend!" The black boulder came bounding toward us, knocking us both down with affection and covering our faces with big slobbery kisses. We had found a new stray. We named him to match his voice—Boom Boom.

Even though he turned out to be full of love and affection, he did have some very odd ways. One of them involved stones. That's what those big holes were all about up in the Cornfield. He wouldn't pick up just any old stone; it had to be a very special light-colored stone. The first sign of a Great Stone-Hunting Expedition was when Boom Boom passed you by, intently sniffing the ground. After he had located the spot where a Great Stone lay, he would stand like a statue, staring at the spot for hours until his back legs began to tremble. If he decided the Great Stone might be underground, he would dig huge grave-size holes, until he found the exact stone, and then go into one of his trances.

On several occasions he decided the Great Stone was on the River bottom. He would swim up and down the River and no one could go boating or swimming until he had dived to the bottom, bringing up his Great Stone. He tied up River traffic for hours. Once the trance stage of a Great Stone-Hunting Expedition was over, he'd ever so gently pick up the Great Stone and, carrying it in his mouth, walk very stiff-legged and serious-like down through the middle of the Village to his Great Stone Graveyard stone piles in the Meadow. There he would add the new Great Stone to the other Great Stones in the pile. Not until this strange ritual had been performed was he the same old Boom Boom again. Tail wagging, full-of-love-and-affection Boom Boom.

Then there was the matter of tents. Boom Boom was wild about tents.

After the Big Snow had melted, we held a special Town Meeting to discuss whether the Town Line could be moved to include the Pines and Big Karl's farm. All agreed to try these new boundary lines. Boom Boom was elected Chief Messenger Runner, to show our appreciation for his saving Fox Glove's life. He lived right in the center of the Pines in a clearing we called Boom Town. It was full of all the tents Boom Boom had carried up from the River banks—pup tents, army tents, even a wigwam. Though there was still a chill in the air, Boom Town was one of our favorite places to spend the weekend. We always slept under piles of blankets in one of Boom Boom's tents and would wake up in the night to be lulled back to sleep by the soughing of the wind through the Pines.

But one night we were wakened by a different sound—a hair-raising howl that soared above the wind, which had shifted to the east. We were frozen with fright. Finally McCragan dared to peek out of the tent flap. There in the center clearing was Boom Boom, with his big black head thrown back, howling his heart out. At first we thought he was having a nightmare. Then we realized the east wind carried with it the smell of the faraway Land by the Sea where Boom Boom had been born. We were at a loss just how to handle his homesickness, until McCragan hit on just the right thing. The only tent he was missing was a circus tent, so we promised we would find him one, never dreaming we could.

Dragonflying

At the northern boundary of the Ford was Denton's Hollow.
That's the long, dark valley where Fox Glove lived. We didn't
go there, partly because dark places gave Lynch the creeps and
partly because of a pirate flag with a skull and crossbones on it
flying at the Hollow entrance. The flag belonged to the owner
of the Hollow, Admiral Del. He had been away on the high seas
for several years. Fox Glove was his caretaker, but we really
didn't know the Admiral and were just a little afraid of him, so
we stayed away.

Lynch, as usual, was the first one to see him return in late
March. Lynch had been fishing for sunnies, when he happened
to look up and see a strange silver object, like a long pipe, sticking out of the water. Startled, Lynch reeled in his line. To his

amazement, the silver pipe moved toward the Ford Landing. Before it reached the Landing, a hump began to rise right out of the water in front of him. The hump got bigger and bigger as more of it emerged. Lynch thought it might be a whale. Just then a trapdoor opened at the top of the hump and a figure emerged. Lynch caught the rope that was thrown, pulling hard to bring the hump alongside the Ford Landing. Out stepped a stranger to Lynch who saluted smartly and said, "I'm Admiral Del." He was dressed in a black sea cape and wore a large three-cornered hat with faded gold braid. The hump had a name, HOAGIE, lettered on her side. Admiral Del said he needed some

help unloading, so Lynch came to find McCragan and me.

We spent the better part of the day lugging heavy sea chests up to the entrance of Denton's Hollow. Admiral Del was firm about not wanting us to step one foot into the Hollow and made it crystal-clear that we were to stay away until we were invited.

After we finished hauling the last chest, he again saluted smartly and gave each one of us a solid-gold doubloon. McCragan was hired to deliver the Admiral's groceries, leaving them at the entrance to Denton's Hollow for Fox Glove to pick up. The only one who went beyond the entrance was Boom Boom, when he had a message to deliver. Lynch was hired to keep an eye on the *Hoagie* when she was, as Admiral Del called it, "in port." We didn't know where he went on his trips and didn't ask questions.

Finally, at the end of April, Admiral Del sent a note by Boom Boom, saying he was leaving immediately for a sea voyage but would we three come for dinner the night of July the Fourth to watch the fireworks display? We sent word back that we would be there, hoping the time until the Fourth would go quickly. We always knew it was the Fourth of July because on that night the Valley echoed with the sound of distant cannonading. Perhaps on this Fourth we'd find out what caused it.

After the frost had gone out of the ground and the flood waters had receded from the meadows, we listened for the first peepers in the Marsh—a sure sign that spring was on the way. Suddenly the fields and woods were carpeted with May flowers, and the nights were getting shorter. It wouldn't be long before the Fourth of July and Admiral Del's party. In the meantime, the River, which was the western boundary of the Ford, was the place where we spent most of the warm months—catching sunnies and catfish, swimming at the Big Buttonwood Tree, fishing at the Mill dam, and on warm summer nights camping out under the Pines. But best of all was Dragonflying.

McCragan, Lynch, and I each owned large inner tubes that Retread Fred had given us in exchange for pumping air at his garage. Together we owned a fourth one that we rigged up to carry supplies. On that particular day, we went to the Mill, rolling our inner tubes along and carrying a basket full of canned sardines, a hunk of Store cheese, a box of crackers, a jug of lemonade, and all the cookies we had been hoarding from the various jars at our disposal. After we launched ourselves at the Mill tail race when the big wheel was running, we had to shout to be heard above the roar from the water rushing over the nearby Mill dam and the rumble of the big wheel. The water bubbled and churned out of the Mill arch, sending us spinning on our way—each on his inner tube, with the spare, carrying the picnic basket, roped behind.

Once the narrow Mill race emptied into the River, we just drifted along with the movement of the current—a slowly spinning, water-level kind of ride, like a leisurely dragonfly. When a willow branch hung low, trailing its drooping leaves in the

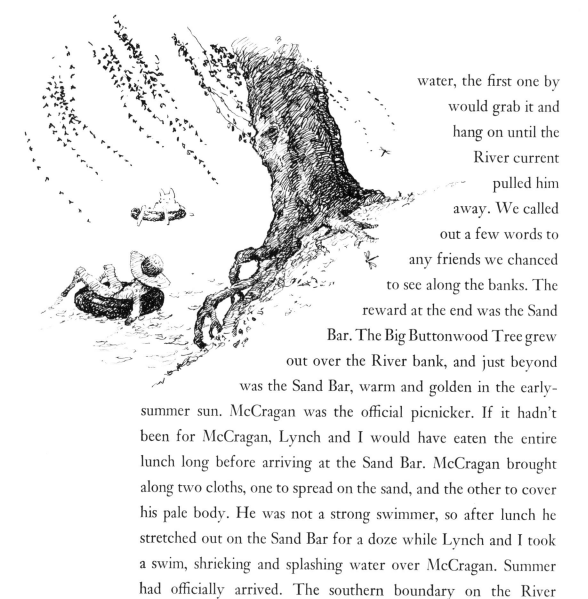

water, the first one by would grab it and hang on until the River current pulled him away. We called out a few words to any friends we chanced to see along the banks. The reward at the end was the Sand Bar. The Big Buttonwood Tree grew out over the River bank, and just beyond was the Sand Bar, warm and golden in the early-summer sun. McCragan was the official picnicker. If it hadn't been for McCragan, Lynch and I would have eaten the entire lunch long before arriving at the Sand Bar. McCragan brought along two cloths, one to spread on the sand, and the other to cover his pale body. He was not a strong swimmer, so after lunch he stretched out on the Sand Bar for a doze while Lynch and I took a swim, shrieking and splashing water over McCragan. Summer had officially arrived. The southern boundary on the River stopped at the Sand Bar, so it was the farthest we had ever gone Dragonflying until that particular day.

Lynch was the one who first gave us the idea of exploring a little downriver below the Sand Bar. It was bound to happen sooner or later, but what started out as a simple dare ended in a series of events that changed all our lives. We vowed we wouldn't go too far, because even Lynch was still in awe of the roaring water he had heard that early morning coming out of the Deep Gorge. I remember, after we had pushed off, how forlorn the spare inner tube looked, sitting abandoned with the picnic basket on the Sand Bar.

I, for one, was a little afraid.

When we rounded the first forbidden bend in the River, I expected a catastrophe, but all was peaceful and placid as before. Two dragonflies flew by, their iridescent wings glistening in the afternoon sun. We moved slowly on, keeping our inner tubes close together, and listened for the distant roar of water that would mean the rapids of the Deep Gorge were nearby. We floated along and even began shouting back and forth, when almost imperceptibly we began to lose control of our inner tubes. A powerful current was pulling us downstream. Just as we heard the noise we had been listening for, I became separated from McCragan and Lynch and was swept around a big bend in the River. The roar was growing louder and louder, but above it I could hear Lynch yell, "Jump off! Quick, jump off!"

I jumped out of my inner tube and saw it spin around and around before it vanished out of sight ahead. I'm a fair swimmer but have never felt a stronger current. My last memory is of being swept into the dark, mist-filled Gorge, where the waters pounded and tumbled in rapids. I woke up wedged between two rocks, the River swirling around me. The steep sides of the Deep Gorge towered above me on both sides. Although bruised and aching all over, I was able to free myself and wade to the narrow shore. McCragan, Lynch, and the inner tubes were nowhere in sight. Inch by inch, wet and shivering with fright, I slowly made my way up the side of the Deep Gorge. When I reached the top, I lay under the trees for a short rest to catch my breath, before I began working my dazed way along the edge. Finally I came to the Gorge entrance.

Somewhere a crow cawed three times. Lynch! My heart leaped for joy. I cawed back and sat down on a tree stump to wait. The caws came closer and closer as I answered. Lynch was working his way toward me. Suddenly there he was, standing beside me. He cautioned me not to speak and motioned upriver, and we silently hugged for joy. Lynch was like a panther in the woods. Not one twig snapped as we silently walked among the tall trees. Again he cautioned me not to make a noise.

Suddenly I knew why. Through the branches I could see a red carriage standing in the dense wood. The light was fading fast, for the sun had long ago disappeared behind the western ridge of the Deep Gorge. But there was enough light left to see a figure pacing impatiently back and forth beside the red carriage, as if waiting for something to happen or someone to appear. A fox head was painted on the carriage door.

The black coach appeared so quickly it seemed to come from nowhere, but its mud-spattered wheels rumbled by so close we could have reached out and touched them from our hiding place in the bushes. They came to a halt. Peering through the leaves, I saw the name CASTLE GRENÂDE, with a fleur-de-lis painted in gold, on the coach door. Perched high on the seat and holding the reins in one hand was a driver dressed all in black, with a sheer mask, like a black silk stocking, pulled over his face and head. We were so close I was terrified. If the masked driver hadn't been distracted by the impatient figure walking toward him, he could have looked down and seen Lynch and me hidden in the thin undergrowth.

The driver spoke. "Make it quick. I have guests waiting for me at the Castle Grenâde for tea."

We could see the other figure more clearly now. He was dressed in a close-fitting scarlet jacket with a black velvet collar. A white stock was neatly tied around his short neck and he wore high shiny black leather boots. "Your guests can wait long enough for us to have a little talk about our speedy flight from the Palace that night."

The masked driver remained perfectly quiet. The impatient one spoke again. "Perhaps I should refresh your memory about a sea voyage we took after that flight."

A long silence. The horses pawed the ground, making the black coach creak. Finally the masked driver answered. "I don't know what you're talking about—all this nonsense about a speedy flight and a sea voyage. I'm not who you think I am."

"Well, well, well, so you're gonna get uppity, are you?" The impatient one's voice changed. "How about if I remind you,

Black-Powder André, alias Baron deFâce, that you wear a face mask because your black powder backfired in your face? I guess you never thought you'd see me again after our ship went down. Well, here I am, ready at long last to collect my debt for helping you to safety that night."

The masked driver's voice grew angry when he asked, "What do you want—money?"

The impatient one squealed his reply: "Money—I've got cider barrels full of that. What I need is class—the kind of baronial class you and only you can give me. I want your baronial blessings and endorsement for the Ambassadorship."

Lynch gasped as the masked driver reached for his long whip to strike at the figure standing below him on the ground, but the driver controlled himself and replied, "You're asking for the impossible. No one in their right mind would choose you for such a refined position."

"Oh yes, they would, if you gave a big send-off reception in my honor and announced me as your personal choice. You seem to forget you'd be rotting in jail if it wasn't for me."

"You're blackmailing me. All right, I'll give you a reception on one condition and only one, that you will never threaten me again. Do I make myself perfectly clear?"

"When will the invitations go out?"

"Immediately."

"Agreed, but don't try pulling any of your Crowning-Blow

Affair tricks on me, 'cause I'll have your Castle Grenâde surrounded. Do you hear—surrounded."

With that, the whip really did crack. The horses plunged ahead and the black coach vanished in the dense woods. The scarlet-coated figure walked, or more like waddled, back to his red carriage. As he climbed up onto the seat, I thought I heard a tiny squeal coming from a large wicker basket tied to the carriage rear, but I was confused by what I had heard and seen that day, and I never gave it a second thought. Lynch led the way to McCragan lying on the grass beside the River, still pale and half drowned.

When it was safe to talk again, Lynch told of their close call after they jumped off their inner tubes. By using every ounce of strength, he had been able to swim to the sinking McCragan. Lynch grabbed him under the jaw and worked his way to a trailing willow branch. He pulled the branch almost to the breaking point and somehow managed to get himself and the half-drowned McCragan up the bank, then fell exhausted on the grass. Together Lynch and I told McCragan about the scarlet-coated figure with the red carriage and the masked driver on the black coach.

McCragan immediately came back to life and asked us questions about the red carriage. It seems it had appeared at McCragan's only last week, but the driver who had come to leave an order for a scarlet riding coat did not fit the description of the figure we had seen striding impatiently back and forth. We knew we had overheard something of a serious nature and vowed that if the red carriage came back to pick up the completed riding coat we would investigate the matter. In the meantime, we would keep the whole experience a secret, because we had ventured beyond the Village boundaries and gone Dragonflying beyond the Sand Bar. We started cautiously on our long trip back to the Ford, staying close to the River. It was pitch-dark when we reached the Big Buttonwood. The moon had risen, and there, sitting forlornly in the moonlight on the Sand Bar, were our spare inner tube and the picnic basket.

Dolly Den Den

By the time we got back to the Ford and said good night to McCragan, it was very late. The Village was dark, except for one light shining from the Tavern window. Lynch went over to see if everything was all right and called, "Look!"

There in the Tavern side yard was a big carriage. We stole up to get a closer look, and sure enough, it was painted red, with a fox head on the door. Then we heard a noise—really more of a tiny sob—coming from inside the basket strapped to the rear of the coach. We listened. Another sob as I unbuckled the strap and raised the basket lid. Just enough light came from the Tavern window to see what was inside. To our utter astonishment, we discovered a bedraggled little piglet in a sunbonnet! Lynch gently lifted it out and that's when I noticed it had a

crooked snout that leaned way
over to the left. My mind flashed
back to that day at Big Karl's—
to another piglet with a crooked
snout in Lynch's arms.

Then came the whispered
question, "Who are you,
piglet?"

A teary answer, "Dolly Den Den."

We found a carriage robe and
wrapped poor Dolly Den Den in it,
for she was shivering from fright, then
quickly left with her on our way toward
the Big Rocks. Toots wasn't very happy about being awakened
in the middle of the night, but as soon as Lynch unwrapped the
carriage robe, she took full charge of the shivering little piglet.
She gave her a hot bath and a good rubdown, while Lynch made
buttered toast and brewed a pot of tea. It seemed to help, for she
asked if we had a cookie. While she nibbled, she told us of her
plight.

She was, of course, Den Den's only daughter, and the youngest
of nine, which made her feel sort of on the tail end of things.
She had never been allowed to wander off that vast Estate of the
Baron deFâce. That morning Dolly Den Den had decided to run
away. She meant it to be just a Little Runaway, but it turned out

to be a Big one. This made Dolly Den Den cry all over again, so I gave her another piece of toast. Her eight older brothers had sneaked out at various times. They came back with glowing tales of the Big Wide World that lay outside. Dolly Den Den decided she wanted to see just a little bit of that Big Wide World for herself.

So, while Mama Den Den was working at the Private Railway Station, Dolly Den Den had tied on her best sunbonnet, slipped out of the house, and started down the path in the woods. It was most exciting, especially when she hid behind a tree when her daddy, the Estate Manager, walked by. That's when she decided to leave the path and just wander in the woods—hoping to reach the edge of the Estate so she could have a little peek at the Big Wide World that lay outside. On and on she wandered, even through a Black Tunnel, looking for the Big Wide World. All of a sudden she spotted a bright red carriage through the trees. No one seemed to be around, so she climbed up one of the big wheels of the carriage to where a wicker basket that looked like a large picnic basket was strapped on the back. Hoping that there might be food inside, she unbuckled the strap. She had just raised the lid high enough to see that the basket was empty when she heard footsteps—so she jumped inside. A terrible moment came when the footsteps reached right up to the wicker basket and the lid was buckled down. This made Dolly Den Den start shivering again, so Toots held her a little more tightly.

She waited and waited. Nothing happened. She peeked out through the tiny holes in the wicker and breathed a sigh of relief —for there was the black coach from the Castle Grenâde coming to her rescue. She would have let out a squeal, but the voices she overheard sounded mad. Instead, she decided to stay quiet— after all, the red carriage would go back to the Castle Grenâde with the black coach and then she'd sound her alarm of distress. Finally she heard the creak of the carriage and knew the driver was climbing up to his seat. That's when Dolly Den Den let out a little squeal of delight. I had been right. That's exactly what I had heard while hiding in the undergrowth of the Deep Gorge with Lynch.

On and on the carriage went, bouncing Dolly Den Den back and forth. Finally it stopped and she peeked out to try to see what was happening. She watched the driver carry a lighted carriage lamp over to a big hollow in a tree. He bent over and brought a box back with him. When we asked her how big it was or what it looked like, she quickly replied that it was most beautiful, it had straps that glittered like gold in the lamplight. She heard him mutter to himself, "After all these years the fool still doesn't know my real identity."

Finally the carriage stopped again, this time long enough for Dolly Den Den to take a little nap, but when she woke up and remembered where she was and how far away she had traveled from the warmth of Mama Den Den's ample lap, she began to cry. That's when Lynch and I heard her. After we had listened to her story, Toots sang her a lullaby and rocked her to sleep. I just wanted to go back home to bed after such an exhausting day.

But not Lynch. In a nonchalant way he picked up a burlap bag—it meant he was going frogging. It was just like him, tired as he was, to go frogging instead of to bed, and I knew the reason why. The next day was the Fourth of July and Admiral Del's fireworks display. Lynch wanted to take him a very special present—a mess of frogs' legs. Lynch was champion frogger at the Ford. He usually liked to go after midnight, when the Marsh was still, with only an occasional sleepy croak being heard. He had an uncanny sense about where to find a sleeping frog in the pitch-dark. With frogging net in hand, Lynch would

work his stealthy way along the Marsh edges, being careful to keep his lantern light turned low. At just the right moment he turned up the lantern wick and directed the beam of light onto the sleeping frog. Startled by the light and frozen with fright, it popped its eyes open. Quick as lightning, Lynch brought his net down. He reached under the net and grabbed a kicking leg, deftly transferring a bullfrog to the gunnysack slung over his shoulder. He hoped Admiral Del would like his present.

The Ship "Roundelay"

In the morning McCragan told us he had looked through his mother's orders and found the riding coat was completed and waiting to be picked up. We spent the day getting ready for Admiral Del's party, and then it was time to go.

Lynch didn't like Denton's Hollow a bit. Like all dark cave-like places, it gave him the creeps. Right away I could see he was nervous, so it didn't surprise me when he cupped his hands over his mouth and yelled, "Hello!" "Hello—hello—hello" echoed back down the Hollow. Lynch yelled "Hello" again, and three more hellos echoed back—then utter silence.

He had just about talked us into leaving the Hollow when a voice, seeming to come down on us from way up high, yelled, "Ahoy, who goes there?"

"We three," answered Lynch, while "we three—we three—we three" came back at us in waves down the Hollow. Silence, then from high above, "Come aboard."

We walked single-file into Denton's Hollow. About halfway, a rope ladder came tumbling down over the side. McCragan grabbed hold and started climbing up. It was eerie, standing there alone with Lynch—not a sound to be heard. Oak trees towered over our heads. He said he had a strange feeling that many eyes were peering down and watching us from hidden places in those rocks. I wondered where Fox Glove's house was located. Lynch was fidgety and I could see he was all for getting out, when a voice yelled down, "Next!" We flipped a gold doubloon. Lynch got crowns. He took a deep breath, grabbed hold of his sackful of frogs with one hand and the rope ladder with the other, and started up the side.

When my turn finally came and I reached the top, it was like entering another world. Admiral Del didn't live in a house at all —he lived on board a three-masted pirate ship that was stranded high and dry under a grove of towering pines. It was painted black and white like the long, thin banners and Jolly Roger that flew from the middle mast. The stern rose up two levels above the main deck, with ship's lanterns mounted on the sides. A row of windows ran across the stern above the big rudder. The sails were neatly furled to the spars, with three crow's nests high overhead, one on each mast. Lettered in gold on her nameboard

was the word ROUNDELAY.
The gunports were all open,
each with a cannon poking through.
Admiral Del stood on the highest level of the
afterdeck in his three-cornered hat, with his great
black sea cape blowing in the late-afternoon breeze. A brightly
colored parrot in a cage called out, "Man the guns! Man the
guns! A boarding party is climbing over the sides!" It's the only
time I ever saw Lynch at a loss. He just stood there, speechless.

A monkey scurried by, carrying the rope ladder under his arm, and leaped nimbly up the side and onto the deck.

Then a stern voice called an order, "Pipe the visitors on board!" Amid the piping of the shrill bosun's whistle blown by the monkey, and the parrot screaming in his cage, we walked up the gangplank that brought us onto the main deck. Admiral Del saluted and took us down the companionway to his quarters below. The cabin was full of strange curios from foreign lands —shields, cutlasses, chairs made from whalebone, big shells, and a shrunken head. The row of windows, slanting across the back, looked out onto a waving Sea of Grass. A ship's lantern hung by a chain over a large round table. Admiral Del politely offered each of us a chair and thanked Lynch most kindly for his present. His tone of voice when he asked us what we had been up to seemed a little bit odd. We flashed each other a quick look. I spoke up and told him we had had a picnic on the Sand Bar. Without a second's hesitation, he snapped back, "You did a little more than that!"

All three of us were aghast. He went on, "Through my periscope I saw the three of you on your inner tubes way beyond the Sand Bar on my way back upriver in the *Hoagie*. You must remember I'm safe in the *Hoagie* and know the River like the palm of my hand. After all the warnings you've heard, I was astounded to see you go so far downriver."

There was nothing to do but face the facts and tell him all about our Dragonflying adventure. Which is exactly what we did. I was going to leave out the part about the strange coach and carriage, but Lynch got carried away and told the whole story. I was sure he would send us back down the rope ladder. Not at all. Over and over again he questioned Lynch and me about the masked driver on the black coach and what we had overheard. Somewhere on board, the ship's bell struck the hour. It was time to eat, so we followed Admiral Del into the wardroom and had an exotic seafood dinner, served by Fox Glove and her children. We had sea-turtle soup ladled from a giant clamshell, and sea snails and deviled crabs. Even a salad made from shore greens, with tropical fruit for dessert. While we ate, we listened to Admiral Del's stories of gales at sea, of mutinies, buried treasures, and sunken reefs.

After it grew dark, Admiral Del said to Fox Glove, "Douse the ship's lanterns. It's time for the fireworks to begin."

When we went back up on deck, far to the south a rocket, with a long fiery tail, climbed high in the heavens, then exploded in a shower of falling stars. Again and again rockets and fireworks illuminated the night sky. From high on the deck of the *Roundelay* it was the most wondrous sight we had ever seen, for we had spent our lives in the Valley, out of sight of such spectacular displays. The Fourth of July celebration ended with a super skyrocket that hurtled higher than the others. When it exploded, seventeen stars drifted slowly to earth, each carrying a letter that together spelled out DEFÂCE BLACK POWDER. Then the dark night closed in.

Before we left the deck, Admiral Del ordered Fox Glove to keep watch and let him know if she heard any suspicious noise. Not for one instant was she to leave her post. Back down in his cabin, he relit the ship's lantern, closed the portholes, and bolted the door. Then and only then he spoke, and his words made my heart pound with a mixture of fear and excitement. "I think you have uncovered part of the mystery of one of the world's most famous crimes—the theft of the Royal Crown of France."

All three of us were astonished and hung on to every word he said.

"We must move with the utmost caution, for our very lives could be in grave danger. These are desperate, ruthless criminals."

He walked over to his large, sea captain's desk, took a key from around his neck, and opened a locked drawer. He brought to the round table a volume titled *The Book of Pirates.*

"Let me give you the background history of the Crowning-Blow Affair."

He began to read aloud.

The Crowning-Blow Affair

"This robbery and explosion remain unsolved. The prime suspect is named André. He was or is medium-tall, slimly built, with long legs and tapering fingers. A distinct way of walking, with his feet turned out. His hair, blond. His eyes, blue. By nature a loner. He showed his ability with black powder while he was still very young. There is reason to believe that his career began on a quiet pond in a public park. A racing regatta was taking place among several toy boats. Suddenly the most elaborate and winning tin battleship struck an underwater mine and blew up just inches from the finish line. André's smaller gunboat won the race.

"Shortly thereafter, the Académie Française was scheduled to open for the fall term. Up until that time, André had been

tutored at home. His parents thought it would be wise to enroll him in the Académie, so that he might make friends and not be so solitary. Exactly one day before the Académie was to open, it was blown up. A mysterious bomb exploded which totally destroyed several rooms, including André's classroom. There were other unexplained explosions that occurred in and around

the Province where this André lived, but those were probably only practice shots for the crowning, big blast of his career.

"The Royal Palace was so vast it covered four acres of land. One night the King and the Queen were seated on the Palace balcony, surrounded by their court, watching the evening display of fireworks in the garden below. Suddenly a bomb exploded with such violence it broke all the glass in the Palace windows and started a fire in the west wing. A flame, like a shooting star, landed on the Queen's feather wig. The Royal Crown and the burning wig were snatched from the Queen's head, revealing her to be totally bald! Not so much as one down feather on her royal head. This embarrassing sight was witnessed by all of her astonished court. The confusion was so great that the fire in the west wing began to spread before a bucket brigade could be assembled to put it out. In the end, after the Queen's lady-in-waiting brought her another wig, it was discovered the Royal Crown was missing.

"The King was out for blood. Warrants were issued for the arrest of André the Bomber and Royal-Crown Thief. The evening event became widely known as the Crowning-Blow Affair. Not a trace has ever been found of the mysterious Black-Powder André the Bomber and Royal-Crown Thief."

The ship's bell again struck the hour. Admiral Del closed *The Book of Pirates*, while up on deck Fox Glove called out, "All's well."

"Now," he said, "comes my part of the Crowning-Blow Affair. At that time I happened to be cruising offshore in my ship when the heavens lit up bright as day and an explosion was heard. Thinking a revolution might have started, I brought my ship in among the shoals of those foreign waters to see if I might pick up a fugitive who needed a quick passage for a price. It always pays to hang around for a while after a revolution starts. The signal is well known along every coast in the world. If you sight a rocket shooting from the land toward the sea, there on the shore you probably will find a would-be refugee. Before dawn the lookout in the crow's nest spotted a rocket in the sky. I sent a launch inshore, with strict instructions to settle all money matters before bringing any stray on board. Matters were settled and the launch was rowed back to my ship. There were two refugees. One was horribly disfigured—singed eyelashes and eyebrows, blisters all over his face; the other was short and stocky and wore black leather boots. Their passage had been paid, so the bosun's chair was lowered and they came on board. No questions were asked about why their only pieces of luggage were a box strapped in gold and a keg that never left their sight.

"We weighed anchor and set sail for the Indies, but a violent storm blew us off-course and my ship ended up a total wreck on the dreadful Cape Hatteras shoals. It was each for himself in those mountainous seas. One fugitive vanished immediately, and the other, when last seen, was clinging to a spar with one

hand while the other arm was held high out of the water with the keg in his hand. Above the tumult of the roaring seas, his voice could be heard yelling, 'I must keep my powder dry!' Then he disappeared from my sight as the spar drifted toward shore and the pounding surf.

"I thought I was the only survivor. Eventually I made my way to Home Port, hoping for a chance to put back to sea. Home Port was buzzing with news of the explosion at the Palace and the theft of the Royal Crown. It was the first time I learned of the Crowning-Blow Affair. Putting two and two together, I began to suspect that the horribly singed and blistered fugitive

or his partner in black leather boots might have been the Bomber and Royal-Crown Thief.

"One day I was wandering aimlessly around the marketplace when I noticed a beggar sitting on the street curb. He had a sheer black-stocking mask pulled over his face and head. Something clicked. The shape of his head was familiar. The way his long legs were crossed rang a bell. Then I noticed a keg by his side. I sidled up, dropped a doubloon in his tin cup, leaned close, and whispered, 'The Crowning-Blow Affair,' in his ear. The reaction was immediate. The beggar jumped up, spilling coins out of his cup, then grabbed the keg and vanished in the market-place amid the cages of squawking hens.

"Soon after that, I went to sea on a privateer, and was away from those waters for several years. When I returned to Home Port with my new ship, the *Roundelay*, all the waterfront gossip was of a certain Baron deFâce and his spectacular black powder. His career was rumored to have begun the day his masked figure —a keg under one arm—appeared at the Front-Street Battery and asked politely if he could have a word with the gunnery officer. No one heard the conversation that took place, but they all felt the force of the explosion that came from the Front-Street Battery. Windows were blown out. Horses bolted and charged out of control through the streets. When the dust settled, the Mayor was seen rushing to the spot. The Governor arrived for a very secret meeting that took place behind closed doors. Any

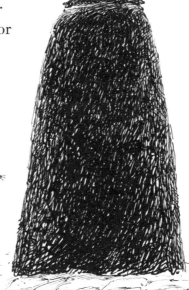

mention of the mysterious blast at the Battery was met with cold stares.

"A month later, the result of the secret meeting was demonstrated at the Governor's Fourth of July celebration. A skyrocket was shot off, and then another and another and another. Never had there been such a spectacular display. The celebration ended with a barrage of bombs so powerful they shook the Governor's mansion and the ground like an earthquake. A masked figure appeared very briefly at the reception and was introduced as Baron deFâce, the inventor of a new kind of black powder. It became world-famous, but he remains a total mystery—seldom leaving his vast Estate or his Castle called Grenâde. He gives lavish parties, which he rarely attends; nothing is known about his past, and no questions are ever asked."

Admiral Del had finished giving us the background history of the Royal Crown, and the part he played in picking up the fugitives. All those years he'd been quite certain that Baron deFâce was the Bomber and Royal-Crown Thief, but he had honored the pirates' code of silence. Now Baron deFâce was being blackmailed by his fugitive partner to gain the Ambassadorship. Blackmail was the lowest form of pirate skulduggery. If we hadn't gone Dragonflying, Admiral Del might never have found out that the second mysterious fugitive still lived.

Up and down the cabin floor he paced, saying over and over, "Something isn't just right."

Then I remembered there really was something we hadn't told him, and that was Dolly Den Den's account of seeing the driver of the red carriage go over to a big hollow in a tree and carry a box back to the coach. Admiral Del stopped dead in his tracks. He came over to the ship's lantern, and his fierce eyes grew even more fierce when he shouted, "What do you mean? Why didn't you tell me? What did she say the box looked like?"

"She said it had straps that glistened like gold in the lamplight."

Admiral Del's fist came down on the round table so hard one of the cutlasses fell off the wall and clattered to the floor, which woke the parrot in his cage, who began screaming, "Treasure box! Treasure box! Treasure box!"

After he'd been given a sea biscuit, things quieted down and Admiral Del said, "That's the exact same box the fugitive carried on board and wouldn't let out of his sight. I remember it well—all strapped in gold. I'll bet you twenty pieces of eight that it holds the Royal Crown. How are we going to find out where this blackmailer lives? How are we going to get our hands on that box to see what's inside?"

It was McCragan's turn to tell him more about the red carriage with a fox head on its door, and the scarlet riding coat his mother had completed. Admiral Del issued an order that we must keep constant watch so when the red carriage turned up at the Ford we could sound the alarm.

It was well after midnight when we climbed down the rope ladder with lantern in hand and walked out of spooky Denton's Hollow. All was quiet as we stole cautiously by the Marsh. Once I thought I heard heavy breathing behind us, but it was only the night wind making its rounds. It seemed to whisper, "Beware of the Royal Crown." None of us felt much like talking. We had too much new information to try to sort out. Our last words when we parted were to meet at McCragan's early in the morning. Perhaps his mother knew when the red carriage would return.

The Land to the North

I overslept. My bedroom was bathed in sunlight when I woke and looked down onto the Village. Something caught my eye. Far up the Valley, a red carriage was winding its way toward the Ford. There wasn't a minute to waste. When I arrived at McCragan's house, he had already left for work at the Store. Lynch was nowhere in sight, but hanging on a hook in McCragan's front room was a brand-new scarlet riding coat. While I was looking it over, I heard the crunch of gravel on the drive outside. McCragan's mother was so busy running the sewing machine she hadn't heard me enter. I parted the curtains, looked out the window, and saw the red carriage pulling up to the house. It had a fox head painted on its door, but the driver, as McCragan said, was not the same one we had seen in the woods.

There was absolutely no doubt in my mind, however, that it was the same carriage.

Without a real plan in mind, I grabbed the scarlet riding coat off the hook, picked up a sewing basket, and slipped outside before the driver had time to tie up the horses. He believed me when I told him it would be necessary to take me to his Master for a final fitting of the scarlet riding coat. It was a wild chance, but I knew there was no other way. I climbed up onto the coach just as McCragan came out of the Store. His face went as white as his apron. Then the carriage pulled away. As we passed Retread Fred's, I spotted Lynch nonchalantly picking over some junk in the Dump. The instant his keen eyes saw that red carriage, he dropped the big spring he was holding, and stood there

bewildered. I raised my hand to give him the signal that all was under control. When we made the final turn that led us out of the Ford, I heard three crow caws echoing up the Valley. That time I didn't caw back. My heart sank when we crossed over the Town Line and headed in the direction of the Land to the North.

The country we drove through was almost without trees. Already I missed the intimacy of the Ford. It was very beautiful, but something was missing. No marshes, very few big woods— just endless rolling hills, with small, fast-running brooks in the valleys. Occasionally my ear caught the faraway sound of a hunting horn echoing across the hills, but we never saw the Hunters. The country was too vast.

The driver became more friendly as the morning progressed, and began chatting about his Master, as he called him. It was Master this and Master that. I found out that his Master had a violent temper and was feared by all who worked in his kennels and stables. Ever so cautiously, I inquired about his Master's background and discovered that the driver knew almost nothing except that his Master had plenty of cash but no class. Whenever he was snubbed by his neighbors, he'd take out his hurt pride by setting off on the chase. The only trouble was that he had overhunted those hills until almost nothing was left for him to chase. The driver had heard his Master mention more than once that he was going farther afield in search of his prey—even going down to the Land to the South of his country Estate. This piece of information sent cold chills up and down my spine, for I realized I was about to meet one of the Hunters we had been hearing north of the railroad across the River from the Ford.

The driver said he hoped his Master was in a good mood, because we were arriving. After we passed through the entrance gates, sleek horses came up to the rail fences that lined both sides of the long gravel driveway, and watched us roll by. A chorus of baying hounds greeted us when we circled the cobbled court-yard and came to a halt in front of a rambling, thatched-roof country house. On top of the stable roof, a gilded fox-head weathervane sparkled in the noonday sun.

There, pacing impatiently up and down the cobbled court-yard, was none other than the scarlet-coated figure Lynch and I had seen in the woods. He demanded to know who I was and why I was there. The horrible moment had arrived and I was scared out of my wits. Cruelty was in his small blue eyes. If I failed to convince him—all would be lost.

I took a deep breath, bowed from the waist, clicked my heels, handed him the neatly folded scarlet riding coat, and said, "Sir, I am the tailor from the Ford. I wanted to be sure that this new scarlet riding coat you ordered would fit."

My heart sank when right then and there he started to put it on, but in the next moment I was saved by the gong announcing lunch. I expected to be sent to eat with the servants, but instead he said, "Come on and get your grub," and marched right past the dining room. I caught a glimpse of it, and noticed the long banquet table was set for a formal dinner, before he shoved me through a swinging door that opened into the kitchen. It had an earthen floor. His Hunters sat at the table devouring their noonday meal. They didn't bother to stand when their Master entered, but kept right on shoving food into their mouths.

I could see their Master led a life of opposites—sleek horses, baying hounds, a cobbled courtyard, and a formal dining room, in contrast to his coarse Hunters and the kitchen with an earthen floor. When our lunch was served, it was a disaster. The leek soup curdled and the spinach soufflé fell flat. The Master screamed at his chef, squealing at the top of his lungs that the chef was fired,

while pieces of spinach soufflé hung out of his Master's mouth.

The chef knew exactly how to calm him down. "But, Master, surely you are too well-bred to let a little matter like curdled soup and a fallen soufflé upset you? Wait until you taste the main course. It's your favorite—hot dogs with sauerkraut."

His Master smacked his fat lips and gurgled with glee. There was no doubt about it—flattery was one of his weaknesses, and the other was hot dogs with sauerkraut.

After lunch, I followed him to the trophy room, where he waddled to take a midday snooze. When I walked into that dimly lit room, I had to restrain myself from running right out again, for staring down at me with fixed glass eyes was Fox Glove's husband, surrounded by hundreds of other fox heads mounted on every wall.

After he was asleep, I stole out to the stables to thoroughly search the red carriage—hoping to find the box strapped in gold. The only thing I discovered was the handkerchief Dolly Den Den had left behind in the big wicker basket. I poked around the tack room without any luck.

Halfway across the cobbled courtyard, I heard squeals and screams coming from the trophy room. "You're fired! Look at my Oriental rug! Get out, out, out, out!" With a terrible crash, the valet came sailing through the trophy-room window and landed head-first on the cobbled courtyard. Dazed, he picked himself up and ran for his life. Inside was chaos. The valet had spilled a bottle of black boot polish on the Oriental rug. Smoke poured out of the kitchen, where the chef was trying to prepare food for the formal dinner being given that evening before the Hunt Club Ball.

Since no one was available to help the Master dress, I offered my services. "Sir, why don't you go up and relax? It's been a tiring day. Take a long, leisurely bath and ring for me when you are ready to dress."

While I waited for him to ring, I searched, with no luck, for the box strapped in gold. The buzzer sounded, summoning me to the Master's quarters. I walked into the mirror-lined dressing room and there he was, all pink and white, fresh out of his bath, seated on a throne chair. I rubbed that pink body down and brushed his stiff bristle-like hair, buffed his knuckles until they shone, and completed the grooming by curling the bleached eyelashes that grew thickly around his small blue eyes.

In his conceit he thought himself maddeningly attractive. Actually, I found him a boar. Before he finished dressing, he hummed a tune and danced a little jig in front of the mirror, clicking his shiny black leather boots together in midair.

> *"Krauty came from an earthen-floor sty,*
> *With brothers and sisters galore.*
> *Now he wears a coat and tie*
> *And will end up Ambas-sa-dor."*

It hit me like a bolt of lightning. Krauty? Brothers and sisters galore? An earthen-floor sty? I stared at him in disbelief. Everything that Big Karl and his friends had told us about the evil raider nicknamed Sour Kraut came back to me. How he'd been born in a thatched-roof sty with an earthen floor. His passion for hot dogs with sauerkraut. How he had become a ruthless boar hunter, with his trophies mounted on the Duke's hunting-lodge walls. How he had escaped with the Duke's treasure box. Admiral Del's description of the refugee who was short and stocky and wore black leather boots. It made me sick when I thought of all those mounted fox heads downstairs. Already Sour Kraut and his Hunters were hunting close to our boundaries. I was dealing with someone who posed a threat to everyone at the Ford, and I must risk everything to bring this menace to a halt. I fought for composure and asked him in a very polite way if he intended to become the Ambassador.

He replied, "I'll fix this horsy crowd. Just because I didn't come from a town house on Pork Avenue, they look down their long noses at me. They won't invite me to join the Hunt Club, so I formed my own hunt. You saw some of my Hunters at lunch today. Aren't they a great bunch? This horsy crowd would never endorse me for the Ambassadorship. Wait 'til they hear tonight who is—it'll knock 'em dead."

The terrible moment came when he tried on his new scarlet riding coat. It fit to perfection. I adjusted his evening tie and gave his black leather boots a last polish before he went downstairs to receive his horsy guests.

At dinner the time came for him to make a toast. He silenced the horse talk by rapping the side of his wineglass. "I want to announce that I'll be running for the Ambassadorship. You will all be invited to the reception that my sponsor will be giving for me. Unfortunately, he couldn't be with us tonight. In his absence, may I ask you to join me in toasting him—my old friend and sponsor, Baron deFâce."

Sour Kraut's prediction had been right. The announcement knocked them dead. After dinner, while I was passing around a box of Cuban cigars, I overheard this remark: "I say, for some time now I've been meaning to put your name up for the Hunt Club. Would you have any objection if I did?"

Sour Kraut flashed me a quick wink and said, "Not at all. Not at all," then poured himself a snifterful of hard cider. He drank so much he passed out on one of his trophy-room chairs, and his guests left for the Ball without him. This gave me another opportunity to search for the Duke's treasure box. I looked behind books and under beds. I poked in bureau drawers and even checked the wine cellar, with no luck. After snoring away for about an hour, Sour Kraut woke up with a start, wondering where he was.

I helped him upstairs and seized my last chance. "Sir, there's something kingly about you. I think it's the royal way you hold your head."

"Me kingly? You don't say. Well, now that you've guessed, I can confide my secret to you. I do have a touch of royal blood."

"Why, sir, I didn't dream! It was just the way you sit that made thoughts of royalty pass through my head."

It worked. In no time at all, he was throwing riding boots,

riding hats, riding coats, and riding breeches out of a closet in his mirrored dressing room. Concealed in the back was a safe built into the wall. I could hear him cussing and muttering over the combination as he spun the dial. Finally the safe door opened. He emerged from the closet carrying a box strapped in gold. He raised the lid and lifted out a crown! I was dazzled by its beauty and knew instantly it was the Royal Crown. It was encrusted with diamonds and rubies that sparkled and glistened in the light. He waddled over to the throne chair and placed the Royal Crown on his head.

In a few minutes he had fallen again into a drunken sleep. I looked longingly at the Royal Crown, now slipping sideways on his head, and then tiptoed downstairs to plan some way to make my escape. I knew I *had* to leave and I also knew that now was my only chance to steal back the Royal Crown. I didn't think ahead about the consequences. The important thing was to get safely back to the Ford before he woke up and found the Crown was missing. With luck, I would have a few hours' lead. I was in the kitchen packing up a little food for my long walk back when I heard three crow caws coming from outside. It was Lynch! Somehow he had come to rescue me.

I tiptoed back upstairs into the mirrored dressing room, ever so gently removed the Royal Crown from Sour Kraut's head, and placed it inside the box strapped in gold. He gave a snort and shifted his position, and I poised to run for my life, but he

was snoring as I stole out of the room with the box under my arm. I crossed the courtyard to the stable, and at that moment McCragan and Lynch came out of the darkness. Their eyes bugged out when I opened the box and they saw the Royal Crown with its jewels sparkling in the moonlight. Then, while we fled like greyhounds through the night, I told them about Fox Glove's husband's end and just who had ordered those traps set in the underbrush across the River from the Ford.

We ran across fields and down the slope of a hill to a little valley where through the darkness I could see the faint glow of a light swinging back and forth. There, lantern in hand, was the outline of a familiar figure—Big Karl, standing beside his delivery wagon. We dove inside the wagon cab with such speed Big Karl never saw the box strapped in gold.

Lynch yelled, "Drive home as fast as you can. We're being chased."

Which was quite possible, for if Sour Kraut had wakened and found the Royal Crown missing, I knew his Hunters would be on our trail in a matter of minutes. It was a hair-raising ride, with all of us hidden inside the delivery wagon. We galloped up and down those hills at full speed. First we were thrown to one side and then the next, until at dawn, bruised and shaken, we reached the first familiar landmarks of the Ford. Big Karl slowed down, which made conversation possible and gave Lynch a chance to tell me how he had maneuvered my rescue. It was a typical Lynch feat.

The minute he spotted me leaving the Ford in the red carriage, he'd flown like the wind over the Hill and down to Big Karl's smokehouse to ask him for help. Lynch confessed he'd told Big Karl a white lie when he said I had been kidnapped by a driver in a red carriage, but it was the only way to get action. None of them knew which way we had gone, but smart Lynch kept wandering all over those rolling hills until he found someone who could tell him where the owner of the red carriage with a fox head painted on its door lived.

We decided the first thing to do was report immediately to Admiral Del. We thanked Big Karl for his help and headed straight for Denton's Hollow to tell Admiral Del our adventure.

The Plan

I opened the box strapped in gold and brought out the Royal Crown—Admiral Del was speechless.

After he had recovered his composure, he said, "Tell me each and every thing that happened."

When I finished, he looked at us with those fierce eyes and warned: "You're in mortal danger. McCragan, get word to your mother immediately that if anyone turns up asking for the tailor at the Ford to say she is the one and only tailor. If he inquires about a scarlet riding coat, tell her to say it was stolen right out of her house early yesterday morning and she'd like it back because it was made to order. Lynch, spread the alarm that the Hunters from the Land to the North are on the chase, and report to me any unusual sounds or sightings. As for you, we have some serious things to talk over."

We sat down at the round table and he said, "I may be a pirate, but there's one thing that will never be on my record—the Royal Crown. Its value is way beyond gold or precious stones. It is the symbol of royalty and must at all costs be returned to France. You've discovered who the Royal-Crown Thief really is, but you've also involved yourself with the most ruthless Hunter in all the world. He'll do anything to get ahead and he doesn't care who suffers for it. I'd be willing to stake my pirate career that Baron deFâce shot off the Crowning Blow but had nothing to do with stealing the Royal Crown. Our job is to get the truth out of him and try to stop Sour Kraut, but it's going to be tricky and extremely dangerous. I need to know the lay of the land on the Baron's Estate. We haven't much time to spare. Someone has to go there immediately to check the place out, but who?"

He began to pace the floor while I wracked my tired brain. Suddenly it came to me. "Widdoes! Of course we'll be lucky if we can find him, because he's all over the place. You see, Admiral Del, Widdoes is still the only one at the Ford who knows how to fly."

"Can we depend on him? This is a serious mission."

All of us knew Widdoes had two weaknesses—his habit of lengthening or shortening the facts, and his tardiness. He was always going somewhere and saying he'd be back in an hour—we might not see him for a week. Once he fell asleep on the limb of the Big Buttonwood Tree, lost his balance, and fell off. When he hit the ground, he said, "I'll be right back."

If you said it took three hours to walk the Town Line, Widdoes would look you squarely in the eyes and swear he could do it in half the time, or the other way around. No matter— Admiral Del agreed to hire him. He sent me off to find him, but it was Lynch who discovered him perched on a limb of an

apple tree enjoying a midmorning snack. Right away he wanted to know what the pay would be, and where did we want him to fly? We told him to meet us at the Meadow on the stroke of noon, that Admiral Del would give him the orders and the terms. We could see that the mention of Admiral Del impressed Widdoes. This wasn't going to be any small-deal flight.

A few of the Villagers stood around, half curious, when they saw Admiral Del stride over to the Meadow, his black sea cape swirling as he walked. But one stern glance from Admiral Del's eyes sent them hurrying on their way. For once, Widdoes was on time. When Admiral Del took a small leather bag from his pocket and poured out a whole handful of pieces of eight, Widdoes's eyes bugged out.

The Admiral spoke in his best Admiral's voice: "Four for now, and four more when you bring back the correct facts. Did you hear me? *The correct facts!* You are to fly downriver to Baron deFâce's. I want you to come in low and take notes on the placement of absolutely everything on his Estate. Don't miss a single thing. We'll be waiting for you at the Tavern no later than four o'clock—not a minute later. Do you understand?"

Widdoes was so carried away he actually gave Admiral Del a smart salute. I'm sure in his mind he was suddenly on the quarter-deck of a flagship. We stood there in the Meadow while he took off, and kept watching until he became a black speck in the vastness of the summer sky. It was a perfect thermal day. Widdoes

told us later that he followed the meandering course of the River and was able to soar all the way down to the Deep Gorge country.

He hadn't been gone more than an hour when a low, distant rumble was heard. Our River Valley is famous for its rip-roaring thunderstorms. Rain beat against the windows of the back room of the Tavern, where we waited impatiently for Widdoes's return. Four o'clock. Four-thirty. Admiral Del had worn a path in the waxed oak floor with his constant pacing up and down.

At four forty-five, poor drenched, bedraggled Widdoes came in.

His flying suit had shrunk up to his
knees and he ran smack into the table,
for his goggles were all steamed. He was
a sight, but when Admiral Del plunked
down five instead of four pieces of eight,
he perked up and told us about his flight.

Even before we heard the warning rumbles,
Widdoes had spotted the great thunderheads building
up on the northern horizon. He knew that long before
four o'clock the storm would hit. Thermals were one thing,
but air turbulence was another. Widdoes had learned from bitter
experience that a broken wing took months to mend. He
was wondering whether to turn back toward the Ford
to beat the storm, and then he reached in his
flight-suit pocket, felt the warmth of those
pieces of eight, and decided to take a
chance. He took out his pad of paper
and made quick notations of this
and that, while the thunder
growled ominously around
his head. On a hill behind
the Deep Gorge

he located the Castle Grenâde, a turret rising between massive stone wings, and terraced gardens surrounding it all.

The most important information he brought was the location of a Guest Palace under tall trees, and the route of the Private Railway that started out at the Station located beside the Track Gates. Widdoes had even caught a brief glimpse of Den Den through the Station window. He thought she looked forlorn and sad—not the jolly Den Den we had known at the Ford. He followed the Private Railway that circled in and around the huge Estate. Sometimes it disappeared into the deep woods, to re-appear on the other side. He noted its wandering route as best he could, for time was running out—the rain was beginning to fall. We drew a map from his notes; poor Widdoes was pretty tuckered out.

After he had left, we locked the door of the back room in the Tavern and sat down at the table. We had just begun a very serious discussion when Lynch motioned to keep quiet. His sharp ears had picked up the sound of crunching gravel. We peeked out the window and in the driving rain saw the red carriage, a fox head on its door, pulling into McCragan's driveway, loaded down with crude, brutish Hunters.

In a flash Admiral Del cocked his pistol, strode over to the window to get a closer look, and said, "There he is, getting down from the driver's seat. No question about it, he's one of the fugitives I picked up off the coast of France!"

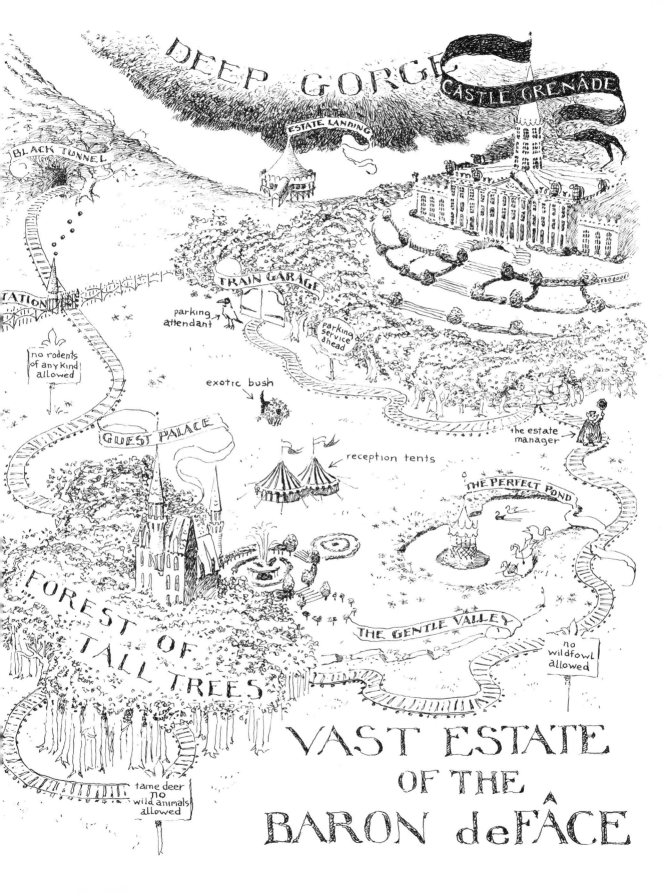

He watched Sour Kraut knock at the door and then stride impatiently up and down the porch floor in his black leather boots. Nothing happened. He peered in a window, then yelled, "Let's break the door in!"

Admiral Del took aim with his pistol just as McCragan's mother opened the door. She spoke to Sour Kraut and handed him a brand-new scarlet riding coat! Muttering something we could not hear, he climbed back on the red carriage and that motley crew pulled out of the driveway, headed for the Land to the

North in the driving rain. McCragan's mother had saved the day by telling Sour Kraut the first coat had been stolen right off the hook early yesterday morning so she had stayed up all night making a new one.

While the rain beat against the windows and the thunder crashed, we sat down at the table to make our plans for entering the Estate of Baron deFâce. Admiral Del would stay home to keep a sharp eye on the Ford and the Royal Crown, which was locked in his sea chest on board the *Roundelay*. Over and over again he assured us that if we didn't return by an appointed time he would come to our rescue downriver in the *Hoagie*.

Ram Tram

The success of our dangerous mission really depended on Lynch, the mechanical genius. His greatest invention was completed but needed a final test run. It was the contraption he was talking about that day we crossed over the Town Line on to Big Karl's farm—a sort of car that would run on the railroad tracks. Lynch named it Ram Tram. It was a most ingenious combination of wheels, pulleys, gears, ropes, and a windmill that operated a ram from an old water pump. We would use Ram Tram to take us on to Baron deFâce's Estate and back home again to the Ford.

I doubt whether Lynch could have built it without Retread Fred, who never threw anything away. There were glorious piles of assorted bodies, engines, wheels, and odd machine parts that he kept around his garage. Next to the Dump, it was

Lynch's favorite source of supply. The only reason it was second-best to the Dump was that Retread Fred liked to bargain. Rightfully so, you never got anything for nothing at Retread Fred's Garage. Maybe he would exchange a gear for a mess of frogs' legs, or a bucket of bolts for a creel full of freshly caught sunnies, or a paper cup of wild honey for a pulley. An extra-special item called for a basket of jumbo eggs.

When he needed them, Lynch knew where to get eggs. He would steal into a hen house in the dead of night and make soft clucking noises like a brooding hen. Quick as lightning, he'd grab up a sleeping bird, and before the hens knew what had happened, Lynch would be gone with a basketful of jumbo eggs. Lynch got some of his best parts for Ram Tram from Retread Fred in exchange for these great big eggs.

The most noticeable feature of Ram Tram was the windmill Lynch mounted on the rear. Toots got it for Lynch by waiting on tables at the Tavern. All her tips for a year went toward getting that windmill. A shaft leading down from the windmill connected to the ram. To start Ram Tram rolling down the tracks, you grabbed a crossbar mounted on an upright pipe, and by pumping back and forth moved Ram Tram silently along the tracks. Gaining speed, the windmill turned and the ram pumped up and down. Only Lynch understood the pulleys, ropes, and gears that connected the ram to the wheels. To slow down, you simply disengaged the ram and applied the brakes, which were two old shoes. Ram Tram's whistle was blown only by Lynch. It issued forth from Kind Tink's bugle. Since he refused to play any more, he had given it to Lynch. We enjoyed hearing the plaintive sound of taps again when it echoed down the Valley.

There were three ways to steer Ram Tram down the tracks. The easiest was to stay seated with your feet on the crossbar, which you worked in the same way you steer a sled downhill. The second way was with a great ship's wheel donated through the kindness of Admiral Del. The third was used only in bad weather. Lynch had mounted a pair of reins on the midsection of Ram Tram which allowed the driver to be undercover in the cab. The reins went out through an opening in the front window and were attached to the crossbar up forward. The cab not only protected the passengers and driver but also served as a sleeping compartment. It came from an old delivery wagon Big Karl gave

to Lynch. He cut windows in both sides and had McCragan's mother make tie-back curtains. The sleeping bunks were a pair of elegant plush seats from an abandoned hearse traded with Retread Fred for three baskets of jumbo eggs. A vase of faded paper flowers hung on the wall. Ram Tram's wheels were one of Lynch's greatest Dump finds. They fit the tracks to perfection.

The next day dawned clear and sunny, just perfect for the Ram Tram test run. About a week before, Engineer Flaherty had turned up in the Ford. We thought he was part of Toots's long-forgotten past. Nothing doing. One day three whistle toots sounded, then three more. Toots was at a Grange meeting and she fairly flew over the hills to the Junction, straight into Engineer Flaherty's arms. He put his stamp of approval on Ram Tram and went along on the test run. Let me tell you, it was a wild ride!

Lynch was mad for speed. Everything was running to beat the horses, and we were hanging on for dear life, when Engineer Flaherty held up his arm to signal a curve in the tracks up ahead. Ram Tram began to tip. McCragan lost his balance and fell off, landing square on his head. Lynch applied the brakes, bringing Ram Tram to a screeching, grinding halt.

We ran back and found McCragan pale and out cold, lying on the side of the tracks. We dashed down the railroad embankment, got a bucket of River water, and threw it over him. He came around all right, but Lynch learned a lesson he didn't forget.

We had gone down the tracks far enough. Engineer Flaherty was convinced that Ram Tram was a huge success, so we disengaged the long pipe from the crossbar, put it in the other end, and started on our way back home to the Ford. A crowd had gathered at the Junction for our return. Midst barks, whistles, and cheers, we came pumping back to the track siding. Admiral Del called for silence. This was a bit baffling to the crowd, until he explained to them the public part of our next day's mission— to enter the lands of the Baron on Ram Tram and return Den Den's tiny daughter. He did not go into details but said it was extremely important that if anyone so much as heard one baying hound or caught sight of a red carriage with a fox head painted on the door to report immediately to him. He had instructed Fox Glove to keep close watch, but he also needed the help of everyone who lived at the Ford. All kinds of wild rumors were whispered about, for they sensed that something serious was afoot.

Tomorrow our whole success depended on getting through the Track Gates. Engineer Flaherty solved the problem; otherwise, we would have been in a real fix. Right after Admiral Del finished his speech, Engineer Flaherty fired up his train. It was hopeless for him to drop off a note for Den Den, because she couldn't read; so Toots made him promise on his honor that he would stop at the Station to tell Den Den we had found her baby. We would bring Dolly Den Den back before noon the next day if she would be sure to open the Track Gates to let Ram Tram pass on through.

McCragan, Lynch, and I spent that long night on board Ram Tram so we would be ready for an early-morning start. Our only problem was Boom Boom—he wouldn't let us out of his sight. He'd run too many messages, and wanted to be in on the action. Try as hard as we could, there was no budging him off Ram Tram—he was there to stay. When morning finally came, Toots brought Dolly Den Den down from the Big Rocks to the Junction. McCragan's mother had made her a dotted-Swiss pinafore and her sunbonnet was freshly starched. She carried a little basket full of acorns—a gift for Mama Den Den from Big Karl. Toots gave her a teary goodbye kiss and we lifted her up on board. Admiral Del had come down from *Roundelay* to see us off. He loaned me his brass spyglass, saying we just might need it, and told us that if we failed to return by midnight he would be waiting at the Estate Landing in the *Hoagie*. Then he wished us good luck. Lynch started pumping. I looked back. There were Toots and Admiral Del waving from the middle of the tracks. I had been apprehensive during that long night but felt much better now we were on our way at last. Boom Boom's ears were flying straight back and he was loving it all as we sailed down the tracks, hanging on for dear life, windmill turning while the ram pumped up and down.

When we rounded a bend, things grew tense on board, for we had just passed the point of no return. A sign read: BLACK

TUNNEL ENTRANCE STRAIGHT AHEAD. Dolly Den Den closed her eyes from fright. The Black Tunnel passed under the River and ended at the Track Gates to the Estate deFâce. Engineer Flaherty had told us it would be clear until noon. Suddenly all was pitch-dark, for we had entered the Tunnel. Lynch started to get the

creeps again. Then the worst thing happened. Boom Boom began to moan and wail—his Yearning-for-the-Land-by-the-Sea, soul-searching, moaning wails. They echoed in a most dreadful, un-nerving way above the clickety-clackety of Ram Tram's wheels on the rails.

Lynch disengaged the ram to slow us down, in hopes that Boom Boom would stop. Nothing doing. He wanted to get off. While we were arguing in the pitch-dark, I reached out to give him a reassuring pat and discovered to my horror that he wasn't there. Lynch lit a lantern. No Boom Boom in sight. As soon as we started pumping, the lantern blew out. We called. Not a sound. There was nothing to do but pump onward, convincing ourselves he had run back to the Ford. His abandoning Ram Tram distressed us all.

Way up ahead, we could make out just a speck of daylight. With hearts pounding, we emerged from the Black Tunnel, our eyes blinded briefly by the bright morning sun. There, smack ahead, were the Track Gates and the Station, which looked like a sentry box, with a pointed roof. Six balloons were flying from the pointed Station roof, with one letter on each that together spelled out DEFÂCE. The Track Gates opened up with a bang and we passed through. Behind the Station window we caught a brief glimpse of a very familiar figure in a stationmaster's hat. Dolly Den Den, who had been sitting on my lap, also caught sight of that big, lovable figure. There was no way to hold her back. She jumped right down off the side of Ram Tram and ran squealing, "Mama Den Den! Mama Den Den! It's me!" The basket of acorns spilled all over the tracks.

Never again do I expect to get such a snorting, hugging, kissing welcome as we all received. We let Dolly Den Den tell her mama all about her Big Runaway adventures—the wicker-basket ride, Toots, and the Big Rocks. We told her we had a dangerous mission to perform on the Estate and needed her help. Could she somehow get us a pass to see Baron deFâce?

She went right over to the Station phone, turned a crank, and we heard her say, "Lovie, they've brought our baby back safe and sound. I'm sending them down the tracks. Give them all the help they need."

She promised not to leave the Station for a second, because we might have to escape in a hurry. We told her if she heard taps on the bugle, to open up the Track Gates. We left Dolly

Den Den in her arms, climbed back on board Ram Tram, and with beating hearts, for none of us knew just what lay in store for us up ahead, we started down the Private Railway tracks.

The Estate deFâce

The fields on either side had already been mowed. Small, neatly lettered signs were posted: NO RODENTS OF ANY KIND ALLOWED. After leaving the neatly trimmed fields, the Private Railway entered a Forest of Tall Trees—oaks, beeches, tulip poplars, walnuts—whose trunks rose up high over our heads, straight as arrow shafts. Not one branch low enough to be reached by a ladder. No limbs for swings or tree houses. No small birds flew. The Forest floor was carpeted with wild flowers, and occasionally a deer stood there like a frozen statue, gazing in wonder at such a strange intrusion on its privacy. More neatly lettered small signs read: TAME DEER—NO WILD ANIMALS ALLOWED.

In the middle of this carefully groomed Forest of Tall Trees the track split Y-fashion. Lynch steered Ram Tram to the right.

I consulted our map and wondered if perhaps he should have gone left, but it was too late. The land seemed to be sloping down into a Gentle Valley, where the Private Railway tracks ran beside a small stream. It was easy to see that it had at one time meandered down through the Gentle Valley. Now it was straightened so that it was a miniature canal. Water splashed over little dams as it flowed down through the Gentle Valley, and flowering shrubs of a kind we had never seen grew in profusion on the slopes. No cattails grew. No muskrat houses. No marsh hummocks. No wild ducks and geese waddled on the closely clipped lawns. This time the small sign read: NO WILD FOWL ALLOWED.

At the bottom of the Gentle Valley was a most Perfect Pond, with white and black swans gliding across the mirror-like surface. Swan boats drifted idly by the shore. On an island in the middle of the Perfect Pond was a sparkling, white, lacy gazebo. When we started up the other side, it was like leaving a dream world. The hills became more rolling. Thousands and thousands of daisies nodded their heads in the summer breeze. This too perfect world made me homesick for the Marsh, the Big Rocks, the Pines, the River, and the Ford, but when I caught sight of Lynch pumping up front, I felt more at home. If only Boom Boom were there.

The hills were becoming more tumbled, the way they were around the Ford. Up and back down we went. It was a stomach-tickling roller-coaster kind of ride. Then there it was before us, a huge Castle of pale gray marble, with the heights of the Deep

Gorge beyond. The Castle wings seemed to follow the contours of the hill, with terraced gardens and grape arbors covering the slopes. A turret rose out of the center of the roof, full of viewing windows, and flying from the top of the pointed turret roof was a long, narrow black banner. Lettered on the long, narrow black banner were the words: THE CASTLE GRENÂDE.

Lynch slowed down to a snail's pace. In the middle of the tracks, straight ahead, was a wall, in front of which stood a uniformed figure. He held a sign that said: STOP. When he strode toward us, we could see that dark goggles covered his eyes and a pistol was stuck in his belt. Without saying a word, he looked

Ram Tram over—then took off his dark goggles. We recognized him: Den Den's husband, the Estate Manager. Out of the corner of his mouth, in a low voice, he said, "Thanks for finding our daughter. Den Den's been out of her mind with worry. This place is crawling with guards, and the Baron is in a state. He's been playing the organ day and night. That's a bad sign. You'd better get going back to the Ford."

We told him we just *had* to see the Baron. It was a life-and-death matter.

"What'll I tell him?"

"Tell him Admiral Del of the ship *Roundelay* has sent him something we must deliver personally," I replied.

The Estate Manager walked over to the Deep Gorge wall, spoke a few words into a tube-like opening, listened for a reply, then pressed a button.

To our utter astonishment, the wall opened up. Lynch pumped Ram Tram inside before the wall closed behind us with a clang, locking us in. We found ourselves in a vast underground cave. The track ran between hundreds of barrels neatly stacked on stone shelves. On each was stamped a skull and crossbones above the words DEFÂCE BLACK POWDER lettered in red. The Estate Manager jumped on board and pointed to a tunnel that led to the right, which brought us abreast of a huge cage. Another button was pushed, and the cage doors opened up. Lynch stayed on board to guard Ram Tram, while I entered the cage with

McCragan and began to move up, up, up, up, up. When the cage doors opened, we stepped out into a dark, oak-paneled long hall where a guard told us to wait.

Great thunderous chords of organ music filled that long hall. The music seemed to come from nowhere and everywhere at once. A massive double staircase led to the Castle chambers above, and from the vaulted ceiling hung a crystal chandelier that swayed with the vibrations from the music. Suddenly the organ stopped. A strange apparition came swiftly toward us down that long hall. The apparition was tall and slim and walked with his pointed black velvet shoes slightly turned out. He was dressed in a handsome black jacket cut in at the waist, with a black turtleneck sweater, and a gold fleur-de-lis on a chain. His head and face were covered with a sheer black silk-stocking mask. There before us was the driver of the black coach that Lynch and I had seen as we lay hidden in the thin undergrowth.

A cultured voice, speaking with an accent, asked who we might be. I answered, "Admiral Del's junior officers."

He turned and we followed him into his library-music room. He closed and locked the massive oak-paneled door.

"Now," he said, "who is this Admiral Del and the ship *Roundelay*?"

I spoke up. "Baron deFâce, I'm sure that you've not forgotten that it was Admiral Del that picked you up off the coast of France?"

"Yes, yes, very good captain—he landed us on the shoals. I could have done better myself. What has he asked you to deliver?"

I handed him *The Book of Pirates* opened to the chapter headed "The Crowning-Blow Affair" and watched him while he scanned the pages.

Through his sheer mask I could see his face begin to twitch, but his voice was controlled when he said, "Interesting story, but what does it have to do with me?"

I knew the moment had arrived for me to lay my cards on the table. A terrible chance, because if I was wrong about the Baron, McCragan and I would probably never see Lynch, Ram Tram, or the Ford again, but there was nothing else to do. "Baron deFâce, we know who you are because we overheard every word of your conversation in the Deep Gorge with the driver of the red carriage with the fox head painted on its door."

During the silence that followed, my heart pounded so hard I thought it would jump right out of my chest. Baron deFâce began pacing up and down that library-music room, stopped, and played a few chords on the organ. We were getting nowhere, so I said it was time for us to leave, but before we did, was there a message to take back to Admiral Del?

"You heard that other blackmailer demanding my endorsement of the Ambassadorship. What blackmailing demands is the pirate Admiral Del requesting?"

My answer gave me pride to relate: "All he wants is the return of the Royal Crown to France."

"And so do I," said Baron deFâce. "Believe me, I had nothing whatever to do with that theft. I'd give anything to know who the Royal-Crown Thief really is. I only wanted to demonstrate my new black power to the King and Queen, but as luck would have it, the fuse was faulty, and you know the rest."

We needed Lynch. Smart, shrewd, clever Lynch would know in a flash whether the Baron was telling the truth or simply calling our bluff. We sent for him and when he arrived we had the Baron repeat word for word what he had said.

Lynch listened very carefully and said, "Tell him about Sour Kraut."

After Baron deFâce heard all there was to tell, he rushed over to the wall phone. "Get me Den Den immediately. Den Den, has a red train car with a fox head painted on its door passed through the Track Gates? It has! Under no circumstances allow it to leave."

He hung up and said, "That blackmailing Crown-Jewel Thief and brutal raider, Sour Kraut, has arrived on my Estate. He's spending the weekend at my Guest Palace because this evening I'm giving him a reception to launch his campaign for Ambassador."

After more stern orders that under no circumstances were we to be disturbed, we went into secret conference behind that locked oak-paneled door to make our plans for catching Sour Kraut and forcing him to expose his guilt to the world. We all agreed that he could be lured to the Ford if we drew a map that purported to show him where the Royal Crown was hidden. McCragan would have to see to it that the map got into Sour Kraut's hands, because if he caught one glimpse of me, all would be lost. We set about drawing the map.

After it was completed, arrangements were made for McCragan to be Baron deFâce's personal valet, supposedly sent over to the Guest Palace as a courtesy to Sour Kraut. It was a role that suited McCragan, with all his polite, mannerly ways, to perfection. Lynch would stay with Ram Tram, just in case something unexpected came up and we needed a means of speedy escape. I was to keep out of sight. Baron deFâce gave me the key to a Secret Passageway that he told me wound through every part of the Guest Palace. I would be able to observe each room from peepholes in the Passageway walls.

On the stroke of five, the Baron walked with us back down the long hall. In front of the cage we thanked him.

He bowed and said, "I shall keep Sour Kraut here to give you a chance to prepare for his arrival at the Ford. Late tomorrow I'll fire off my largest rocket to signal his departure from my Estate. Tell Admiral Del to pick me up at the Estate Landing in the *Hoagie* after you've heard it go off. In the meantime, my deepest thanks, good luck, and au revoir."

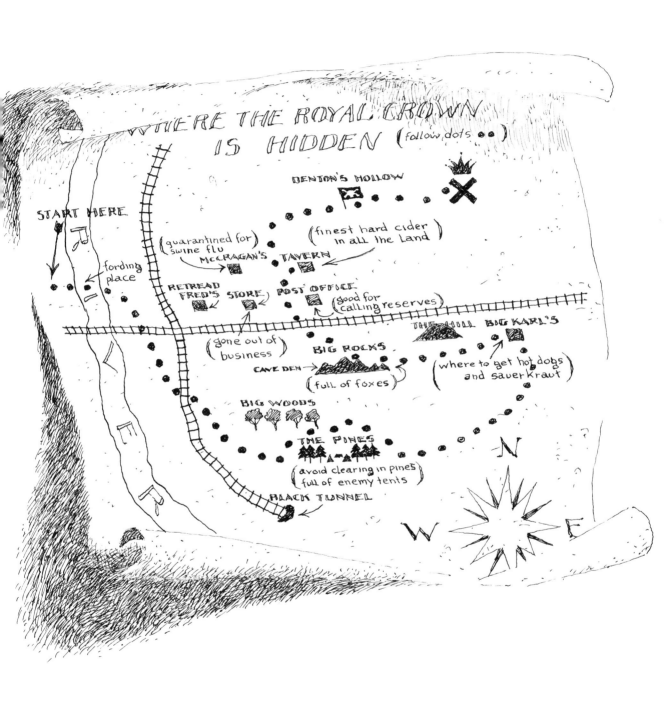

Thunderous chords came from the organ as the cage descended to the underground cave. The doors opened up and Ram Tram, with Lynch pumping, passed on out.

The Guest Palace

We continued on that Private Railway up hill and down. Lynch
was beginning to wonder where to park Ram Tram when we
saw a sign: PARKING SERVICE AHEAD. We approached wide doors
built into the side of a daisy-covered hill. Beside them, standing
at rigid attention, was the Parking Service Attendant. We showed
the parking pass the Baron had given us, and again doors slid
open, allowing Lynch to pump Ram Tram into the Baron's
Private Train Garage. Lynch went out of his mind. The Private
Train Garage was full of every sort of custom-built train car.
There was a Rolls-Royce, a Stutz Bearcat, a Duesenberg, and a
Bentley, just to name a few. Each had special wheels that ran on
tracks! On every door were crests with tiny initials. One train
car was black with a gold fleur-de-lis. The Stutz was racing

blue, with a black crest. Another pale blue one had foreign plates with lions rampant on the door. A small calling card left on the front seat read: THE AMBASSADOR PLENIPOTENTIARY. But the one that caught all our eyes was red with black leather seats. The emblem on the door was a fox head, and glued to both bumpers and a wicker basket on the back were stickers reading: FOR AMBASSADOR—YOU NEED ME.

Ram Tram looked like the poorest of poor church mice amid all that elegance. We threw a big piece of canvas over it, said goodbye to Lynch, and promising to meet no later than six-thirty at the Perfect Pond, left in search of the Guest Palace. We wandered from garden to garden, keeping a sharp eye out for Sour Kraut. Suddenly there was the Guest Palace, four stories high, rising up out of the Forest of Tall Trees. It was surrounded by formal gardens with fountains that splashed into marble pools. McCragan and I walked up a curving drive, followed a narrow footpath that wound around to the rear, and entered the Guest Palace kitchen wing totally unnoticed. That big kitchen was a beehive of activity. Last touches of frosting flowers were being squeezed onto dainty bite-sized cakes. Miniature cream puffs were being filled. Baskets and birds' nests of spun sugar hung drying on tiny hooks. Two life-size ice swans were getting final grooves put on their icy tail feathers. Plump sweetmeats were being rolled in sugar, and long strands of dough braided into wreaths. Huge copper kettles full of cold soups were having a

touch of this or that added. Hams, cold salmons, and pressed ducks were being elaborately glazed. Each and every kind of chef was hard at work. The lesser kitchen help were polishing silver and shining crystal. A long-legged grasshopper kind of creature was arranging flowers. Every once in a while he would leap back, clasp his tapering fingers together in ecstasy over his

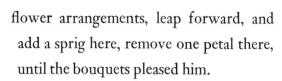

flower arrangements, leap forward, and add a sprig here, remove one petal there, until the bouquets pleased him.

We were totally ignored in all this hustle and bustle, until a very formal butler inquired if we were the outside help.

We said, "Yes, we are to attend to the Guest of Honor's every wish and need."

He told us to go to the servants' quarters and put on our livery. Things were working out exactly as Baron deFàce had planned. I helped McCragan into a brocade cutaway, velvet knee breeches, and a striped vest. He was the perfect valet, and so carried away with the role that he even glued a beauty mark on his left cheek. The Secret Passageway door was exactly where the Baron said it would be— hidden behind a bunch of brooms in a back closet of the servants' quarters.

I turned the key

in the lock, the door opened, McCragan bowed and said, "The Perfect Pond, my Lord, at six-thirty."

My last words were, "Be careful. We're on our own."

I started winding my way down the Secret Passageway. Here and there on both Passage walls were peepholes. I peeked into the kitchen we had just left and saw the French chef licking frosting from a bowl.

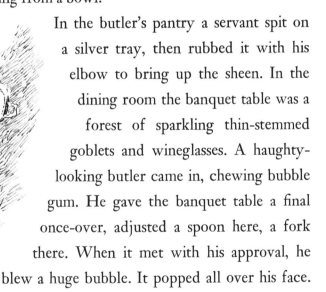

In the butler's pantry a servant spit on a silver tray, then rubbed it with his elbow to bring up the sheen. In the dining room the banquet table was a forest of sparkling thin-stemmed goblets and wineglasses. A haughty-looking butler came in, chewing bubble gum. He gave the banquet table a final once-over, adjusted a spoon here, a fork there. When it met with his approval, he blew a huge bubble. It popped all over his face.

When I reached the marble-floor entrance hall, I realized the guests were beginning to arrive. I was so distracted by all these goings-on that

McCragan and Sour Kraut had almost slipped my mind. I hurried up the Passageway steps that led to the Royal Suite, and sure enough, when I peeked through the peepholes, I saw Krauty in his undershorts jumping up and down in one of his fits of rage, screaming, "My bath water is cold!"

McCragan flew into the room, carrying a heavy bucket of steaming-hot water. He looked a bit harassed. I could see that already the beauty mark had slipped down his cheek, and it landed on his chin as he emptied the steaming bucket of water into the bathtub and sprinkled in some bath salts. The next time I looked, just Krauty's head was sticking out of his bubble bath. I could tell by the pallor of McCragan's face that he was ready for the kill.

In his smoothest voice he said, "Sir, someone just slipped this message under the door. Should I open it?"

"What does it say?"

McCragan answered, "For the Royal-Crown Thief. I'll leave it here on the dressing table for you to open."

Sour Kraut shot out of the tub, his pink body swathed in bubbles. He slipped and went sailing across the marble-tiled bathroom floor. There was a terrible crash when he hit the chiffonier. A book end toppled off and landed squarely on his head, knocking him out cold. McCragan seized the opportunity and left. I followed his hasty exit as best I could, down the flying spiral staircase to the entrance hall, through the crowded reception room, and out onto the terrace. It was time to leave the Secret Passageway by the broom-closet door. I slipped from one formal garden to the next, carefully keeping out of sight, as I made my way to the far end of the terrace, hoping to find McCragan.

An hour later, through an opening in the hedge, I saw Sour Kraut, with a big, nasty-looking bump on his forehead, holding court, but I lost sight of him when he moved inside the larger of two reception tents. Both tents were scalloped all around and striped pale blue and gold, with banners flying from their twin peaks. Something caught my eye. I didn't have to look twice to recognize the face peering intently at the reception tents through the exotic blooms of a bush. It was a very familiar face. Boom Boom

was in one of his trances. I knew disaster lay ahead, but it was too late. At that very moment the string quartet began to play and Boom Boom began to howl—his Great-Yearning-for-the-Land-by-the-Sea kind of howl. Those moaning wails rose all the way up to the very top branches
of that Forest of Tall
Trees,

circled around every corner of the Guest Palace as faces began looking out of windows and guests came pouring out onto the terrace through the French doors. Then Boom Boom made his attack on the reception tent, emitting fierce growls as he tugged and pulled at the ropes. The larger reception tent began to sag, while out of it ran Sour Kraut, holding the bump on his forehead. When he caught sight of the growling, yanking, tugging Boom Boom, his small blue eyes started right out of his head. He began screaming at the top of his lungs, "Mad dog! Mad dog! Mad dog!"

As the reception tent collapsed to the ground, McCragan appeared from out of nowhere, the picture of calm in the midst of chaos. Together, we gathered up the blue-and-gold-striped tent and ran pell-mell with it toward the Perfect Pond. Boom Boom, barking furiously, guarded the rear, but everyone was too stunned to chase us. There was Ram Tram waiting with Lynch at the crossbar. After we jumped on board, Lynch began pumping like he never pumped before. It wasn't easy to get Ram Tram started uphill, so we all jumped out and pushed it up out of the Gentle Valley. Soon we were flying through the Forest of Tall Trees.

When we looked back, we could see a shouting crowd in pursuit. Lynch put his bugle to his lips and sounded taps to signal Den Den of our approach. It wasn't necessary. She was standing at the Track Gates with Dolly Den Den in her arms. She wanted to go back with us to the Ford. There just wasn't time to argue, so we let her have her way. Halfway through the Black Tunnel, we all began to sing:

> *"Pump, pump, pump Ram Tram*
> *Quickly down the tracks,*
> *Merrily, merrily, merrily, merrily,*
> *Den Den's coming back."*

Just before we reached the Junction, Lynch announced our approach by playing taps again on his bugle. All the Ford were there to greet us, and a thunderous roar of applause went up when Den Den emerged from the cab, holding Dolly Den Den in her arms. Again there wasn't time for a real Den Den home-coming celebration, for we had to call an emergency Town Meeting to be held at the Store.

The Capture

So many turned up we had to move the Town Meeting across the road to the Tavern, where every room was packed to overflowing. Fox Glove came down from Denton's Hollow with her children. Toots held hands all during the Meeting with Engineer Flaherty. Kind Tink brought along his newest stray and introduced him to everyone. Retread Fred came rolling three brand-spanking-new inner tubes to replace the ones we had lost in the Deep Gorge. McCragan's mother brought along her sewing—a tiny muumuu for Dolly Den Den.

Admiral Del rapped the butt end of his pistol on the oak table and asked Toots to open the Meeting. At long last she recited her poem "The Dove of Peace," from beginning to end, which seemed most appropriate in view of the events which lay ahead.

Then Admiral Del told about our adventures in the Deep Gorge, my trip into the Land to the North, and the background history of Sour Kraut. The three of us told about our Ram Tram trip onto the Estate of Baron deFâce and described the map we had drawn to lure the evil raider, despicable Hunter, and Crown-Jewel Thief, Sour Kraut, to the Ford.

When we finished, everyone began talking at once. Widdoes kept saying he could do this or that in half the time, so Admiral Del sent him off on a night flight to alert Big Karl's friends to be at his farm the next day because a criminal fugitive from the Old Country would be passing through the Ford.

After Widdoes had put on his flight suit and goggles and taken off from the Meadow, we made a long list of things to do tomorrow so we would be ready and waiting for the arrival of Sour Kraut. All were eager to get to work.

Admiral Del closed the Meeting in a most solemn way: "A real enemy will be coming to the Ford, so I expect each and every one of you to do your duty. Good luck and good night."

By late afternoon the next day, Retread Fred had rigged up an engine that, once started, never stopped backfiring. They hauled it up to the Big Rocks, where it sounded like a rifle battery placed along the Ridge. Boom Boom pitched the circus tent in the Pines. He replaced the banners with two flags reading: BEWARE OF MAD DOG. His duty was to relay news of Sour Kraut's approach to Headquarters on the Hill. The Tavern Keeper was told to put a handful of knockout pills in the barrel of cider at the Tavern. A big sign on the Store said: CLOSED—GONE OUT OF BUSINESS. A second, on McCragan's front door, read: QUARANTINED FOR SWINE FLU. The Post Office was open for business, but hidden in the outgoing-mail box was a rat trap with spring set, just in case Sour Kraut wanted to send out a letter calling for reserves. As for the Royal Crown, it was still inside the box strapped in gold, safely hidden in Admiral Del's sea chest on board the ship *Roundelay*.

Everything was planned in detail. Lynch and McCragan dug a big pit at the Cave Den entrance and covered it with branches to conceal a mesh-hammock snare. If a pack of hounds swarmed over the branches and fell through, the snare would be triggered. All day long, wagon after wagon arrived at Big Karl's farm, filled with his friends armed with brooms, clubs, and cudgels. Widdoes had, as usual, been carried away and told them a whole army of fugitives from the Old Country was attacking the Ford. As it turned out, he was correct. Inside Big Karl's barn was Den Den, just roaring to get started with the battle.

She kept pawing the barn floor, muttering, "A-one and a-two and a-three and a-four."

She wouldn't let Dolly Den Den, who was all dressed up in a new muumuu McCragan's mother had finished during the night, out of her sight. Every detail was completed by the time the sun set. A hush fell over the Valley as all ears listened for the signal that would announce Sour Kraut's departure from the Estate of Baron deFâce. On the dot of seven-thirty, a tremendous explosion echoed across the hills, coming from the Land to the South. Engineer Flaherty, stationed at the Junction, laid his ear to the tracks. Sure enough, something was approaching. We all flew for cover. Seconds later, around the bend came a red custom-built train car with a wicker basket strapped to the rear. It went roaring by, with Sour Kraut bent over the wheel, and disappeared up the Valley in the gathering dusk, headed straight toward the Land to the North.

The time had come for Admiral Del to leave on the *Hoagie* to pick up Baron deFâce at the Estate Landing. After he cast off, we sat around the Ford Landing waiting for his return. A feeling of excitement filled the night air. We waited and waited in the dark. At last we realized what we thought was a bullfrog croaking in the Marsh was Admiral Del's foghorn blowing because the River was shrouded in mist. We lit lanterns and Lynch played taps on the bugle to help guide Admiral Del to the Ford Landing. When the *Hoagie* emerged through the mist, we could see the masked figure of Baron deFâce on deck, surrounded with barrels of black powder and boxes of fireworks. He was introduced all around.

We pitched in and helped carry the barrels and boxes up to Denton's Hollow. When we finally said good night, the ship *Roundelay* was taut with sea law and order. Every gunport was open, every rocket cannon ready to fire, with barrels of black powder and boxes of fireworks held in reserve. Now there was nothing to do but wait. It was a long, long night. I kept waking up, thinking I heard a train car rumbling down the tracks, or the far-off baying of hounds.

Word came before dawn. One of the night-wandering patrollers brought a message to Boom Boom. He'd been swimming upriver and seen campfires in the night. He said he had slithered up the bank, peered into the enemy camp, and discovered a whole crowd of scarlet-coated Hunters sleeping on the ground.

Curled up around the bonfires were packs of hounds. Sour Kraut was not coming alone. Lynch ran from battle station to battle station, cawing like a crow, to give the alarm. By daylight, when the sound of a distant hunting horn echoed up the Valley, we were ready. Widdoes put on his steel helmet, took off from the Meadow, and circled low. Upon landing, he reported that the

crowd of scarlet-coated Hunters
stretched back in the hills for
a mile! He took off again to
see if reserves were bringing up
the rear.

Before he had time to report back, we
heard a second hunting horn echoing across
the hills. It was much closer than the first,
and followed by the baying of hounds. If Sour
Kraut was using the map we had drawn, he and his army would
soon be crossing the River and skirting the Pines. Sure enough,
Boom Boom came panting into Headquarters a half hour later to
report that a pack of hounds had sniffed around his circus tent.
He had let out his most ferocious growl, opened the circus-tent
flap, and bared his teeth, and they had gone off, yipping, with
tails between their legs.

Through Admiral Del's spyglass we saw the Hunters come
swarming into Big Karl's seemingly deserted farmyard. One of
the Hunters dismounted from his horse. I could tell by the way
he waddled that it was Sour Kraut. My hunch had been right;
he was inquiring at Big Karl's smokehouse for hot dogs with
sauerkraut. All the scarlet-coated Hunters watched Sour Kraut
walk to the barn with Big Karl. Inside, Den Den blew her
whistle, which was the signal to open the big barn door. Out
poured all of Big Karl's friends, led by Den Den snapping a car-

riage whip. Sour Kraut ran for his life out of the barnyard as fast as his short legs could carry him, with Den Den in hot pursuit. Horses reared and pitched scarlet-coated Hunters clean over fences.

It was total confusion, with yelping hounds, and Hunters chasing after their runaway horses. Den Den caught up with Sour Kraut and carried him by the seat of his riding pants to the big kettle full of steaming water. It was gratifying to watch. But enough was enough. The time had arrived to interfere, before Sour Kraut ended up boiled and roasted, with an apple in his mouth. Lynch picked up his bugle and played taps. Den Den obeyed the cease-fire signal and went trotting back into the barn. Smart Lynch realized Sour Kraut might suspect that he was being led into a trap and flee, so he ran down the Hill and helped him catch a horse. He told us later that the lump on Sour Kraut's forehead had turned a nasty black-and-blue. Lynch said that when he helped him remount, the small pig eyes got even smaller as he growled, "This hunt better be successful, or I'll run all of you through!"

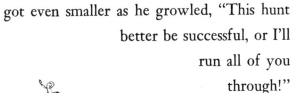

The Hunters reassembled as best they could and galloped up over the Hill, dangerously close to Headquarters. They headed straight for the Big Rocks. We listened. Retread Fred's engine began to backfire. When Sour Kraut reached the Cave Den, expecting to find it full of foxes, the only sounds heard from within were shrieks and squeals. He came back out empty-handed and stood at the Cave Den entrance alongside the open pit. Hanging from a tree limb overhead, a mesh hammock full of hounds yelped. His pink face went purple, positively purple, with rage as he jumped up and down. Then he rode off, full gallop, in the direction of the Village. When he walked into the Tavern to join the Hunters, who had gone on ahead, he found them strewn all over the Tavern floor—out cold from the Tavern Keeper's knockout pills dissolved in the cider.

After that, there was only one Hunter left . . . the ruthless Hunter and Royal-Crown Thief named Sour Kraut. Even though he was all alone, he would not give up and kept taking the treasure map out of his pocket to follow directions. One had to admire him for that. While he was in the Tavern, even his horse ran away, so he started out on foot toward Denton's Hollow in his final effort to locate the Royal Crown. When he passed by McCragan's house, he peered at the swine-flu-quarantine sign, which made him walk a little faster up the Valley. At Headquarters on top of the Hill, we waited and listened for Lynch's signal that Sour Kraut had

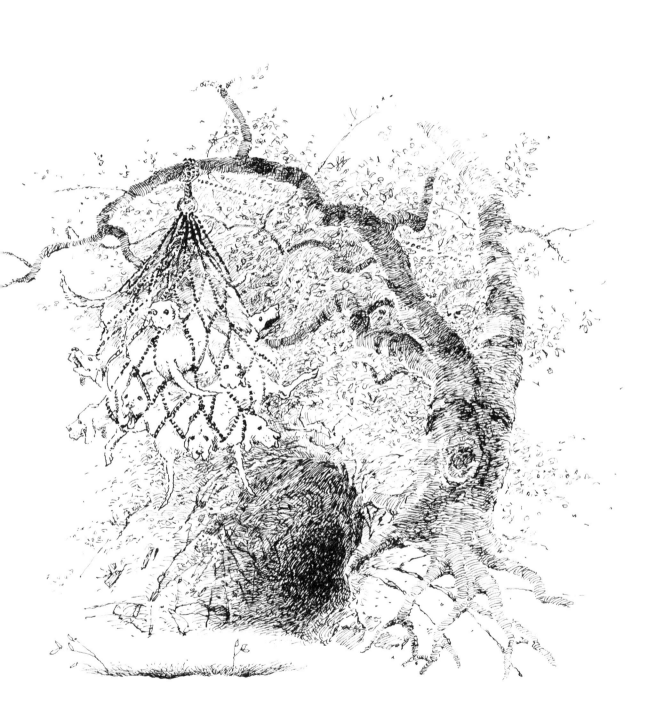

right over the top of the Big Woods! Jeepers creepers, what a ship!" Everyone was impatient for a look through the spyglass, but pretty soon the spyglass wasn't necessary, for there, sailing along on high through the cloudless, blue summer sky, was a full-rigged clipper ship—her big sails billowing. The brisk afternoon breeze carried the Air Ship right over the top of the Hill. We could see a name, *André*, lettered on the stern, and the goggled pilot riding in the balloon boat basket that was suspended from ropes below the Air Ship's sails. Widdoes kept flying around and around the *André* in a lackadaisical fashion, as if a flying clipper ship were an everyday occurrence in the summer sky. I must say, I never before saw Widdoes fly with such grace, showing that Air Ship that he could do banking turns and triple soars in a way no Air Ship could ever hope to do. The goggled pilot turned out to be Den Den's husband, the Estate Manager. He threw a rope over the side of the huge boat basket and we tied it to one of the pine trees that grew atop the Hill.

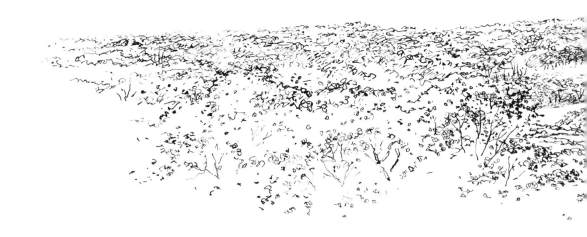

Retread Fred and Lynch ran downhill to Big Karl's barn and lugged back a plank that they leaned up against the Air Ship's boat basket so that Den Den could walk up on board. We all shoved and pushed her up the gangplank, and handed little Dolly Den Den up after her. The Estate Manager began throwing sandbags overboard, which lightened the load. Then he untied the rope, and Den Den was airborne. Dolly Den Den let out a loud squeal of delight, for at long last she really *was* going to see the Big Wide World with her parents. We were green with envy but too polite to tease for a ride, so instead we gathered in two-by-twos and marched down through the Ford —a small parade on its way to the victory celebration on board the ship *Roundelay*.

What a victory celebration it was! When all of us had gathered on board, the ship *Roundelay* almost capsized from overcrowding. Baron deFâce said later that never, never in his whole life had he ever, ever had a better time. There is no question about it, shipboard does have a way of bringing everyone closer together. When the Estate Manager landed the *André* down on the Sea of Grass and Den Den was safely on board the ship *Roundelay*, the Baron announced that he wanted each and every one of us to take an Air Ship ride.

Up in the air and down again the *André* went, each time taking a different route. At last it was McCragan's turn. He was gone longer than the rest. When the *André* brought McCragan

back, he seemed a bit distracted, as if he had something really
serious on his mind. Admiral Del listened attentively while he
whispered in his ear, then rapped the butt of his pistol on the
deck rail and called for silence. McCragan stepped forward and
told us he had sailed up in the direction of the Land to the North.
For the first time he had been able to look down on our River
winding through the rolling hills on its way to the Ford and
beyond to the Deep Gorge country. He followed as best he
could the winding, zigzag route that we had taken in our escape
with the Royal Crown. On his way back,
something that he had been looking
for caught his eye. There, far below,
was a tiny figure stumbling, falling,
getting up again, trying to cross
a plowed field. McCragan dropped
down to a lower altitude. His hunch
was right—the figure was none other
than Sour Kraut trying to reach
the safety of his thatched-roof
country house.

We all cheered and
clapped, but McCragan
held up his hand to
silence our applause.
He told us he landed

the Air Ship just a few feet from the stunned Sour Kraut. In fact, he was so dazed McCragan said it was like leading someone blind across that plowed field when he helped him climb up into the Air Ship's boat basket hovering a few feet off the ground. The Air Ship boat basket? The Air Ship boat basket? A low murmur ran through the crowd, but McCragan continued, "I've brought him back to face your Court of Justice."

The murmurs quieted; all was still. Then a shuffling sound was heard—someone walking with agonizing effort up the gangplank of the ship *Roundelay*. All heads were turned, all eyes watched as the tattered, torn Sour Kraut stepped on deck. He was a sight, for there he stood, his scarlet jacket torn to shreds, one black leather boot missing, black powder marks all over his face, and not so much as a blade of hair left on his head.

He bowed his bald head in shame and began to speak. "I'm licked. I'll be the laughingstock of my neighborhood. I've probably even lost any chances of winning the Ambassadorship. I know I've been a vain, selfish, arrogant boar. All my hounds and Hunters have fled. If I promise never to hunt again, will you forgive me and let me go free?"

Not once did he mention the Duke's treasure box strapped in gold or that he had stolen the Royal Crown. It was time to carry the sea chest up on deck. Admiral Del handed the key to Baron deFâce, who opened it, took out the box strapped in gold, lifted the lid to reveal the Royal Crown, and said, "Have you seen this before?"

A thoroughly humiliated Sour Kraut slumped to the deck and sobbed for mercy. Admiral Del announced that it was up to Big Karl and all his friends from the Old Country to decide Sour Kraut's fate. While the Court of Justice was being held, I slipped away and took a stroll out under the grove of tall pines. That's where Baron deFâce found me. He thanked me again for my part in what had happened and invited me to take a long, leisurely night ride in the *André*. Now that he could return home to France, he wanted to pay for the rebuilding of the Royal Palace. We strolled back and joined the others on board the ship *Roundelay*, for the Court of Justice had reached its decision.

Sour Kraut would be sent back to the Old Country to pay for his crimes. He would leave on board the *Hoagie* at dawn with Admiral Del and Baron deFâce on the first lap of their long journey back to France to return the Royal Crown. When evening came, we shot off all the remaining fireworks to celebrate our total victory, and then it was time for me to climb up into the boat basket of the *André*.

Admiral Del presented me with his brass spyglass just before I cast off, and said the strangest thing: "This is to help you, on your search through life, to reach those distant horizons ahead."

Leaving

Everyone waved goodbye as the *André* lifted off the ground and soared up to become part of the star-filled evening sky. Fireflies sparkled in the Marsh as I drifted silently across the land. When the moon rose, there was the River moving on its silver way toward the Sea far, far, far beyond. Mist rose up out of the Deep Gorge and I could hear the roar of the water, while beyond, the marble walls of the Castle Grenâde glowed spectral-like in the moonlight. On and on I sailed and finally was lulled to sleep by the swaying of the boat basket.

When I woke up, I realized the *André* had drifted far out over the Sea. The first inkling of trouble ahead appeared after the moon went down and lightning flashed across the horizon. A sense of foreboding filled my being and made me wish I had stayed with my friends back home at the Ford. Within minutes the wind began to blow and the rains came. How many days it rained and how far I was blown off-course I'll never know, but finally the skies cleared and the winds blew fair toward home. When I neared the coast, something on the distant horizon caught my eye. I looked through Admiral Del's spyglass and saw a three-masted ship plowing through the waves. I took a closer look, and there from the middle mast was a Jolly Roger blowing in the wind. The decks seemed to be crowded, but I was too far away to see who was on board.

On and on it sailed, until I was close enough to look down on the deck at the upturned faces of all my friends, except one.

Admiral Del yelled up at me through a speaking horn: "The River was flooding at the Ford, so we changed plans and we're *all* on our way to France. Come down on board."

I yelled back: "Where's Lynch?"

"He stayed behind to wait for your return."

Just then a gust of wind hit the *André* and carried me toward the coast. The last sight I had of the ship *Roundelay*, she was headed straight for the open Sea toward France.

By noon I reached the Ford and brought the *André* down onto the Meadow, but no one was there to greet me. The Ford was a ghost town. Evidences of the flood were everywhere: trees uprooted, the Meadow grasses flattened, and Kind Tink's rocking chair hanging from a limb. I rushed up to the Big Rocks,

cawing like a crow, but no crow cawed back. When I reached
the Pines, there sat Boom Boom's empty circus tent, with two
flags that said BEWARE OF MAD DOG on each peak. All was silent
except for the soughing of the wind through the Pines. It was
when I walked alone into spooky Denton's Hollow and yelled
"Lynch!" and "Lynch—Lynch—Lynch" echoed back that I
began to feel apprehensive. I climbed the rope ladder to the top
and found an empty, blowing Sea of Grass where the *Roundelay*
once stood under the grove of towering pines.

The Marsh was the only place left to look, and that's where I
found Ram Tram, swept off the tracks by the flood. It looked
so forlorn and out of place, upside down in the cattails. He was
lying a short distance from it, still dressed in his Road Knight's
outfit. My heart ached when I realized he'd taken a chance and
waited too long for my return. I lifted him up gently and carried
him back to the Village.

At first I thought I would bury him
up in the Big Rocks, but then I
remembered the hours of pleasure
he had in building Ram Tram,
so I decided he would rather
be over near the Junction,
within sight of the Dump and
Retread Fred's Garage. The vase
of faded paper flowers and a wheel

from Ram Tram mark the spot. By sundown my task was completed and it was time for me to start on my way down the tracks, with Admiral Del's spyglass under my arm.

So ends this story of the Ford, where so many of us once lived. It is dedicated to the one who stayed home in the end— to a very special Stray and my closest childhood friend. His name was Lynch.

F I N I S